Pearls on a String

JANE MERLING

Pearls on a String

This book is a work of fiction. Keep in mind that names, characters, places, and incidents either are products of the author's imagination or are used fictitiously. Any resemblance to actual persons, living or dead, business establishments, events or locales is entirely coincidental.

Published in Canada by BayMar Publishing 2022
www.baymarpublishing.com

For questions and comments about this book, please contact us at info@baymarpublishing.com

ISBN 978-1-7780887-8-0 (paperback)
ISBN 978-1-7780887-9-7 (hardcover)
ISBN 978-1-7780887-7-3 (electronic book)

For those who came before us to show us the way

CONTENTS

PART ONE

Chapter One

MY GRANDPARENTS

My grandparents died in the early 1960s, more than twenty years ago. My grandmother passed first, and it was a devastating blow to my family. I was thirteen at the time and being my first experience with death, I was troubled and perplexed about the whole thing. She was the quintessential Grandma— always happy to see and fuss over us. She was an extraordinary cook. Her specialty was primarily German cuisine, as German was her heritage. However, she was also surprisingly good at Italian cuisine as well. No one has ever come close to making lasagna like she used to.

I realized as I grew older that we never completely get over the loss of a loved one. Grief does fade, but the memories stay there, just waiting to be triggered at unexpected times.

She had a stroke. Funny word, I thought at the time. One I would associate with the stroke of midnight or a stroke of lightning, not the taking of someone's life. But that's what happened, one minute she was there and the next she was gone.

Another oddity was that we all got new clothes which were usually reserved for special occasions like Christmas, birthdays, and back to school. I was starting to really enjoy new clothes and the whole shopping experience, but this just felt wrong.

Visitation the evening before the funeral was horrible. I wandered around the funeral home and heard people make comments like, "The family will get closure." The only closure I wanted was to have the casket closed; I couldn't bear to see my grandmother that way. Some people said, "She looks so natural." I didn't think so. Natural was her in the kitchen with her apron on, whipping up delicious meals for us. There was nothing natural about seeing her this way. My grandmother loved birthday parties. We always got to choose the menu for our birthday, including what kind of birthday cake we wanted, and she would bring out hats and decorate the table. She would hide some coins in the cake batter, and we all hoped we would find one in our piece of cake. If my mom or dad found one, they would give the quarter or dime to the birthday person, but we would have to earn it by telling a joke or singing a song.

We had just celebrated my brother's birthday a few weeks before and mine was next. I didn't know how I would get through a birthday without her.

I sat beside my father the next day at the service, and I could feel the tension in him as he sat very still with his hands clasped in front of him. I spent most of the service staring at my new patent leather shoes. I really wanted to love them but couldn't quite bring myself to.

My grandfather was sitting at the end of the row beside my brothers, and at one point I felt my father glance his way. Dad stiffened and his jaw tightened. My grandfather had no real expression on his face. He certainly did not look like someone who had just lost his wife.

Whereas my grandmother was warm and kind, my grandfather was sullen and cantankerous. He never really interacted with us kids and to be honest we were a bit afraid of him. He wasn't particularly mean, just disconnected, and disinterested.

As kids, we accept the people in our lives as they are, largely because they are there when we arrive, full-grown and wearing the mantel of '*parent*' or '*grandparent*.' What else could they possibly be? I took for granted that these elders had always been that way and it certainly never crossed my mind to think about my grandparents, or parents for that matter, in any other way than as I had always known them. I never wondered about their past, or what their younger lives had been like.

There was a lunch provided after the funeral and we adjourned to the basement of the church. The women were scurrying around putting out sandwiches, pastries, coffee, tea, and juice. There were a lot of people there and again I took in bits of conversation. The atmosphere was decidedly different— more relaxed, lighter. People milled around with small plates of food in their hands or sat at tables and told stories about my grandmother. With the selfishness of youth, I thought my grandmother belonged to me and my family, but I learned that she did things for other people as well. She would have probably been one of the women seeing to other people's comfort at times just like this one. It made me feel good. I noticed my grandfather sitting at a table in the corner with a few other men, a cup of coffee on the table in front of him, saying nothing with a very dour look on his face. I wondered what he was thinking.

I wasn't completely oblivious to my family's dynamic. I would spend the night with my grandparents occasionally if my parents were going to be out late. One such time, at about the age of eight, I observed that my grandparents did not share the same bedroom. I remember asking my mother about it. She told me that children should be seen and not heard, so that was the end of that discussion. But telling me to mind my own business only piqued my interest in the matter.

Another thing that had been obvious was that my grandmother was a tall woman for her generation, slim and rather stately. My father is over six feet tall, and my brothers and I have the height gene, too. But my grandfather was short, (shorter than my grandmother) and stocky. Curious things that I had observed and tucked away.

I have two older brothers; Dave is the eldest, good at sports, loves animals, and anything to do with camping and the outdoors. Mike is the middle child, artistic, and an amateur photographer who has a knack for capturing very different and unique pictures.

We were busy teens, and all had part-time jobs as well as school, so often only saw each other in passing as we pursued our individual interests. But our parents had a firm rule that we all had to attend family dinner on Sundays. As well as hosting birthdays and other special events, my grandmother had often invited us for Sunday dinner at her house for no reason other than that she enjoyed cooking for all of us. She left a void in our Sundays when she died that we didn't quite know how to fill. My mother could put on as good a meal as anyone, but I think she enjoyed a break from cooking on those Sundays.

My mother worried about my grandfather being on his own and insisted that he be invited to our house for Sunday dinner. He owned a shoe manufacturing business and my father worked for him from the time he was a young man. My grandfather was a harsh taskmaster, and my father would often come home tired and downtrodden. He had to see him every day and wasn't crazy about having him over for dinner every Sunday, but my mother won out in the end.

The first few Sundays were very awkward. At my grandparent's house, my grandfather had kind of faded into the woodwork as we all enjoyed my grandmother's company, but at our house, he stuck out like a sore thumb. Not to mention that he was a constant reminder that my grandmother was no longer with us. But over time we accepted his presence, and it became the new normal that he was there even though he contributed very little to the conversation or rarely complimented my mother on the meal or thanked her for the invitation. My mother always sent him home with enough leftovers to last a few days, so she felt she was doing her part to keep him fed.

This went on for almost two years until one afternoon I came home from school to find my mother pacing the floor in obvious distress. I learned that my grandfather had collapsed in the factory that afternoon and had been rushed to the hospital. My father was still at the hospital, and she was waiting for word from him. It wasn't good news; my grandfather has suffered a massive heart attack and there was nothing the doctors would do for him.

My grandfather's funeral was much more subdued than my grandmother's, but there was a lot of commotion afterward. Being an only child, my father inherited everything. He spent weeks meeting with lawyers and there was a lot of discussion about what to do. My family lived in a rented house throughout my childhood. My grandfather had not been known for his generosity and did not pay my father enough to buy a house in those days. They insisted that my mother's income from her part-time job went into education funds for my brothers and me, as my parents were big on education and wanted us to have opportunities that had not been available to them. My parents talked about selling my grandparent's house, but my mother liked it and it was larger than the one we were renting, so in the end, we moved into it.

The house had become quite stale with only my grandfather living there so my mother gave it a thorough cleaning, removed the heavy drapes that hung at the windows, and got rid of some of the old furniture. Then she arranged to have the inside of the house painted and it took on a new life. She also updated the kitchen with some new appliances and had a few of the cupboard doors replaced with glass inserts. No one said anything about the kitchen, but I think she wanted to reinvent that space as her own after so many years of it being my grandmother's domain.

Dave finished high school and wanted to become a veterinarian. He planned to work for a year or so to help pay for his education, but now my parents were able to send him right away. He left shortly after for the University of Guelph to pursue his degree, so, other than on certain weekends or holidays, he never actually lived in my grandparent's house.

My father carried on the business for a few years until a group of investors approached him wanting to buy the building. Imports were starting to put a lot of pressure on the shoe industry; the investors had no interest in the business but wanted the property. My father said it was the best thing that ever happened to that business.

The sale of the factory improved things for my family yet again. Mike was finishing high school and he wanted to go to Montreal to study graphic art. My parents had many discussions with him about moving so far away, but that was what he wanted, and in the end, they were able to afford to see him fulfill his dreams. Mike lives up to his status as the middle child and has always been a bit different from the rest of us.

Chapter Two

CHANGES

THE GROUP OF investors who bought the shoe factory wanted the property as part of a vision they saw for the area. To Dad, the factory was a large old building made of brick and mortar, well-worn and showing its age, but they saw the potential for many small manufacturing concerns that would make the district appealing—these businesses could be cloistered together rather than here and there around the city. They felt it would attract tourists as well as locals who could buy specialty items made on site.

As Dad knew every inch of the building, the investors offered him a position as a consultant to the start-up businesses. But first, some things had to be done, such as contracting new zoning laws and renovations to the building. It turned out that Dad had a knack for dealing with city officials and planning boards and as he knew the building so well, he was the ideal person to work with new tenants. Over the years the old shoe factory became home to a glass-blowing business, a tannery, pottery shops, independent jewellers, and many others. Even a modern blacksmith shop that made one-of-a-kind signs and ornaments in rod iron. The area took on a new life and became home to restaurants, seasonal outdoor markets, and live entertainment.

What had once been little more than a place where Dad logged many long hours, became a new and exciting world for him and he was happier than he had ever been. He once told me that where the 'old girl' had once worn plain sensible shoes, she was now stepping out in fashionable high-heeled sandals. I laughed at Dad's metaphor but had to admit that he was right. Eventually, he no longer worked exclusively for the investors. Word of mouth had gotten around, and many others turned to him for advice. A consulting business that he operated for many years was suddenly born.

Dave met Sherri during his first year at the University of Guelph. She was a fellow student, studying business administration, and right from the beginning they did not look to the right or the left of each other. They knew they were meant to be and married right after graduation. They now live in Mississauga with two kids and a Golden Retriever named Molson. Dave worked for an older veterinarian in his small animal clinic for years but when the owner decided on retirement, Dave purchased the business from him. Sherri runs the business end of things while Dave tends to the animals.

Mike stayed in Montreal after earning a degree in graphic arts and shares a loft with Marc, a chef, and part-owner of a popular downtown restaurant. I knew my family pretended that Mike and Marc were roommates, but the reality is that they are much more than that. HIV and Aids were in the news a lot, which was a big concern, but no one talked about that.

I stayed at home with my parents until I obtained an accounting degree and secured a job in one of the big firms. Seeking independence, I moved to a downtown apartment and struck out as a modern young, businesswoman. I thrived in my professional life but stumbled badly in my personal life. I met Ron at a party and thought he was charming and charismatic, the center of attention. He is an advertising executive and was born a salesman. Our relationship moved fast and furious and within a year we were married.

The things that attracted me to him became the bane of my existence. Too late, I realized he always needed to be the center of attention and saw me in a supporting role. He moved us into a condo on the 20th floor of a building filled with glass, chrome, and black leather. I came to think of it as the 'ice palace.' He brought people into our life that served a purpose for him but faded away when he no longer needed them. These people had no substance as far as I was concerned, and I did not form any lasting relationships.

He had an expense account that covered his wining and dining with clients, so he just handed the bills over to the firm. He expected the same of me and at times I was overwhelmed by his spending. His Machiavellian ways shattered our relationship.

I settled into the owner-managed business sector of the accounting firm and fell in love with my work. My clients are people I admire, those who put their heart and soul into making what they love into a viable business. These people are hardworking, and good at what they do, but often struggle with the financial end of things. I help them set up financial plans, arrange leases, accounting practices, and many other things to make their life easier. My husband criticized me for this, calling these businesses small time. Most of them could not afford the fees his firm charged and so, of course, they were of no use to him. As much as he belittled what I did to help these businesses navigate the world of finance, he expected the same from me in our financial life.

I compromised far too much in our marriage and it started to frighten me; I was afraid that I was getting lost in the muck and settling for something less than what I wanted, needed, or deserved. I knew I had choices and had to act on them before I settled into a life I did not want.

Someone left a newspaper on the table in a small café where I was having a solo lunch one day. It was open to the Ann Landers column, and I read it as I ate. One of the letters was from a young woman living in a marriage with a domineering spouse. Ann's advice was to decide if she was better off with him as a subordinate or without him where she could live the life she wanted. I took her advice vicariously and decided I was better off without my husband.

I had negotiated a low-interest mortgage on the condo, and it had gone up in value over the few years that we owned it. My half of the equity and a good income allowed me to buy a small home on the Beaches.

Chapter Three

THE BEACHES

My husband thought I was crazy to give up his lifestyle and he told people that, but I was beyond caring what he or his current friends thought of me. I loved the Beaches. It had the feel of a small town with lots of little indie shops, pubs and cafes, and a boardwalk along the lake. I bought a bicycle so I could ride or walk all over the area. I shopped in the stores and knew many people by name. I was situated a short walk to the beach in one direction and the streetcar in the other for a quick ride uptown to my office. No more travelling underground on the subways for me!

My house was nestled between larger homes but was cozy and comfortable. It was a bungalow with a front porch that spanned the width of the house and a small garden in the back. It had a center hall design with a living room to the left, a wood-burning fireplace, and built-in bookshelves on each side. French doors opened to a small dining room across the hall. The kitchen was directly behind the dining room with white cabinetry and updated appliances. All the windows had been replaced except for the two front ones, thank goodness, which had leaded glass. I loved that house at first sight and knew it was the place for me.

My parents came to see my little house and we walked on the beach to admire the lake. They asked me if I was okay and accepted that I was now a single woman again. They were concerned parents, but not overbearing. They sacrificed for us, as most parents do, but had never been good at sharing their feelings. I remember thinking there was a lot more to my parents than met the eye. The line between my parents and me had always bobbed and weaved. I wondered on that day if I would ever really know them as Rauf and Diane, rather than Mom and Dad.

Among other things, the Beaches have provided me with new friendships. I was walking on the beach on a spring day shortly after moving in and came upon a woman my age with a young boy gathering stones. It was a cool day, but sunny. We were virtually the only people on the beach.

"Hi." I smiled, noticing that they had a small bucket and the young boy (about age six) had run ahead as he spotted something on the beach.

"We're gathering stones and sea glass," he said as he held up a small piece of glass of a milky blue colour. He carefully put the piece of glass in the bucket and held it out for me to investigate.

"Wow," I said, examining the contents of the bucket. I took out a few pieces of sea glass and held them up to the sun. He peered into the bucket and picked out a few more pieces of glass and stones besides. We examined them together and remarked on the size and shape of each.

I straightened up and said, "I'm Sarah."

The boy looked at his mother and she gave her head a slight nod. "I'm Joey and this is my mom, Ro."

"Ro?"

"Her name is Rosemary, but everyone calls her Ro," Joey said matter-of-factly. "Are you new here? I don't think we've seen you before," Joey continued, rummaging in the bucket. "The sea glass and stones wash up on the beach. Some of it comes all the way from China, I think."

"Yes, I moved into a house on Gerard Street a few months ago," I replied, smiling at him.

"Oh, I know the house," Ro piped in. "It's the one with the wide front porch. We live just around the corner."

Our chat on the beach evolved to tea at her house, where we warmed up over a steaming mug. Ro is a vivacious woman with unruly brown curls, big brown eyes, and a personality as popular as a basket of warm puppies. Her son Joey is just like her.

She is an elementary teacher at a school in the Beaches and is very popular among families with young children in the area. Our friendship developed quickly, and we share a mutual admiration. One Sunday afternoon in September we were chatting on my porch.

"Tom is talking about getting married," she said, sipping her diet coke.

"Oh, how do you feel about that?"

"I'm fine with it, but a bit concerned about Joey. Tom is a good guy, Sarah."

I knew that from the few times I met him based on the way he interacted with Joey when he picked him up or dropped him off.

"Do you have feelings for Tom?"

"Yes, but not romantic feelings. We were a couple of flakes back in the day. I had been teaching for a few years when we met and had grand plans to go off to Europe or somewhere to teach for a few years. He was working construction and he would work just long enough to make enough money to take off for weeks at a time. When he ran out of money he would be back, pick up a job, and the whole cycle would start over again."

"We had fun in those days, but neither of us was ready for a commitment. Getting pregnant with Joey was a complete shock to both of us. I lost my parents in the car accident the year before (she had already told me about that) and my brother and I received a settlement, so I was all set money-wise to travel even if I didn't get a teaching job."

"I thought long and hard about getting an abortion, but I just couldn't do it. But getting married simply was not in the cards for us. So many of the kids at school are from broken homes, Sarah, and it's not hard to see how difficult it is for them, especially the little ones. Joey never has been or will be a mistake. After all, he is the most amazing creature on God's green earth."

We laughed. "That he is," I agreed.

"So, I used the settlement money to buy my house, instead of trotting off somewhere. It was hard at first, but Tom and his parents helped a lot. They are the only grandparents Joey has and they love him to death. Tom's mother has told me that Joey made a man out of Tom. He owns his own construction company now and has become a responsible employer as well as a supportive father."

"Do you think Joey will adjust to Tom getting married?"

"Well, he knows Grace, Tom's girlfriend, and seems to get along with her. Joey knows he lives with me but spends time with Tom and his parents. He hasn't gone through a separation because Tom and I never lived together."

"Yes, he is a happy, well-adjusted kid. You and Tom can take credit for that."

"Someday we'll explain all this to him, in an age-appropriate way, and we'll answer his questions honestly when he asks, but for now he seems fine with everything."

"Hmm, I think that's a good way to handle it, Ro."

"What about you, Sarah, what happened in your marriage?"

I was thoughtful for a moment. "You know those comments you hear about people sometimes?"

Ro looked puzzled. "Things like 'that woman is fabulous at what she does, but she has no clue how to present herself,' or 'that guy is brilliant, but he's a social moron.'"

She laughed and nodded.

"Well, I was one of those people. I mean I am good at what I do professionally, but I was a different person in my marriage." I told her about the 'ice palace' and how phony and self-centred my husband had been.

"He wanted a Stepford wife, but with benefits—I brought a good income into the mix. I wanted equal billing, a partnership, someone to share my life with, not to be subservient to his wishes. He had no empathy or compassion for things that matter to me. I don't think he ever asked what matters to me."

"I can't picture you as a Stepford wife, Sarah." Ro looked at me closely.

"I felt trapped. From the outside it looked like we were a successful young couple, enjoying the good life. I was embarrassed to admit even to myself, that I had been sold a bag of magic beans by someone who only had his own interests at heart."

"What finally made you decide to get out?"

I told her about the random newspaper at that café and the Ann Landers column. She frowned for a few minutes and then burst out laughing. We had been in a serious conversation for over an hour and suddenly Ro was laughing hysterically. I was startled, but then I caught the bug, too.

The two of us were howling with laughter on my front porch on a beautiful Sunday afternoon. Mrs. MacDonald, one of the long-term residents from down the street was walking her dog.

"What are you girls up to?" she asked, laughing too. "Are you drinking wine up there on that porch?"

"No," we assured her, holding our sides, "but we could be if you'd like to join us."

"Thanks, but I'd never get my dog walked if I started that at this hour." She waved as she continued down the street.

"Speaking of wine?"

"Sure, why not."

When I poured the wine and placed some snacks on the table Ro said, "You could have your pick of men, Sarah. You're gorgeous with that height and slim figure. I wish my hair would lay smooth the ways yours does." She patted her own riot of curls.

"Maybe," I said, "but I'm in no hurry to get attached to anyone right now. I'm enjoying my independence. Besides, I'm not sure the type of man I'd want even exists."

"If you find him, make sure he has a brother for me!" Ro laughed and continued, "I've seen you coming home from work looking very professional, but never uppity. And today in jeans and a tee shirt with your hair in a ponytail, you look amazing. Everyone in the neighbourhood likes you and Joey loves you!

Kids are very perceptive, Sarah. They like when you spend time with them. You go bike riding with us and look for stones and glass on the beach. That day Joey gave you the flowerpot with sea glass and stones glued all over it, you acted like it was the best present you've ever received. And when he spilled juice on your rug, you didn't get mad. No, you're a natural person, there's nothing phony about you.

And what you've done with this house is awesome. It is so inviting and comfortable. You must have asserted yourself in the end."

"Well, Ron may be a good salesman, but I'm a great negotiator. I hired a lawyer—a woman, and we hammered out a fair deal. After all, I paid for most of it while he was spending money on himself."

"Poor Ron," she said sarcastically. "I'm sure he'll find a way to sell his magic beans to someone else."

"He made a pass at my lawyer," I said straight-faced.

Ro laughed again. "To Ann Landers," she said.

"To us taking off for Europe someday," I replied.

Chapter Four

ZIPPER AND THE GANG

RO LEFT SHORTLY after to be home for Joey. I carried our wine glasses and snack plates into the house. I paused in the hallway noticing the late afternoon sunlight streaming in through the windows. It cast a soft illumination over the rooms and puddled on the wide planks of the pine floors. The condo had big windows that let in lots of light, but it was different there as it bounced off the hard surfaces. In this house, it was soft and floated around the rooms.

As I continued through to the kitchen, I heard some commotion from the den. I found Zipper at the patio door wanting to come in for his dinner.

My backyard is small, but it has a patio that is shaded by a large maple tree and a hedge along the back and on both sides. There is a patch of grass and flower beds filled with shade plants like periwinkle and lily of the valley. A shed, sitting on a cement base is located at the back of the yard against a hedge. It stays dry inside, so I use it for storage and the few garden tools I need including a push mower which James, at *Back in Time* sold me. I was putting it away one day when I heard a rustling in the hedge.

Startled by the noise I took a step back as a beautiful cat made its way through the hedge. We did a stand-off for a few minutes, each appraising the other. He looked as startled as I was and after a moment's hesitation, he took off back through the hedge the way he had come.

I saw him again a few days later and after that, he started hanging around my garden. I asked around the neighbourhood about him and even tacked up signs at the greengrocers and a few other shops, but no one seemed to know him. He was not wearing a collar, so it appeared he was homeless.

I started putting out food for him. At first, I left it on the patio, but every day I moved it a bit closer to the sliding doors in the den. He would show up in the late afternoon, eat his dinner but then disappear again. He showed no signs of being concerned that I kept moving his food closer to the house. It became a little ritual that we performed every night, and I looked forward to seeing him.

Zipper, the cat, was a real stunner and must have had some Maine Coon cat in his DNA as he had the characteristic slightly pointed ears and long fur in shades of black, caramel, and white through his body and bushy tail.

One night it was pouring rain when I got home so I filled his dishes but put them just inside the patio door which I left slightly ajar. I went about preparing my own dinner and eventually, I heard the screen door open. Peeking around the corner I saw that he had managed to open the screen door just wide enough to slip through and was contentedly enjoying his dinner. After that, he came into the den every night and it wasn't long before he started to explore the rest of the house. Everyone knows you can never own a cat, but we became roommates. I bought him a collar, special food and water dishes, and a brush.

I knew we were in for the long haul when he jumped up on my lap one night and let me brush his luxurious coat. I borrowed a carrier and took him to Dave in Mississauga for a checkup. Dave said he was a bit undernourished, but primarily in good shape. We estimated his age to be about five years old.

Dave and I both wondered why he was a stray as he didn't appear to be a feral cat, but I never did find out where he came from. He sleeps on a pillow on the blanket box at the end of my bed, but is an outdoor cat and likes his freedom, so every morning he heads out for the day's adventures.

I learned not to leave the door open for him when I discovered a dead mouse that he brought home as a gift for me. After that, he needed to announce himself, and only after careful inspection, was allowed in the house.

I was thinking about Ro as I prepared Zipper's dinner. I was astonished at how quickly I felt like I was able to confide in her. She is completely guileless about her own life, so she invites that kind of confidence in others. Even though she has a lot of support, it isn't easy for her to be a single working mother. But her kids at school love her and she is an excellent mother to Joey.

She introduced me to the Froggy Bottom pub which was a popular meeting spot on Friday nights. The Frogs has a laid-back atmosphere and serves good pub grub and inexpensive drinks. There is a group of regulars, but Ro only goes when Joey is with his dad.

John and Dana lived together on the Beaches and sometimes Dana would be there on her own if John was working. John is a firefighter—a big burly guy, trim but muscular. He had sandy-coloured hair and freckles and is the jokester of the group, but if I were trapped in a burning building, he'd be the guy I'd want on the scene. Dana was his polar opposite, petite with dark hair in a pixie cut. She worked in the real estate division of a law firm on Bay Street and handles all their transactions. She was smart, ambitious, confident, and outspoken. She came to see my little bungalow and asked me outright how much I paid for it and when I told her she said I did all right. They seemed like an unlikely pair, but they obviously adored each other.

Dean lived a bit further downtown, but he and John were in the same firehouse. Dean was Greek with a last name that no one could pronounce. He was not as big as John, but wiry and strong. He had olive skin and dark hair and was quite attractive. I invited Linda, a friend from work to join us; she and Dean hit it off and started dating, so sometimes they were there together and other times she is on her own, too. Linda was Chinese and they made a striking pair.

Katie, a teacher at Ro's school would often show up with her husband Ian. They were the yuppie couple. Both were attractive, well dressed, and soft-spoken, but they can cut a rug when the occasion warrants it.

You never knew who would be there on any given Friday night, but whoever showed up would guarantee to help create a great end to the work week. Nick was the owner, and his daughter Jane waits tables. One Friday night she told us she was opening a gift shop down the street. We all groaned but she said she would still work at Frogs some Friday nights.

"Who else can keep you lot in check?" she said, gaining cheers from all around.

Someone asked if she had a name for her new shop. She said she had some ideas but had not yet settled on a name. With that, Nick rang the bell at the bar and declared whichever table came up with the best name would get a free round of drinks.

The challenge was on hand for the next half hour everyone tossed ideas around, but our table won hands down.

Jane's Fonda Gifts became a reality in time for Christmas shopping.

My parents and I left on the afternoon of Christmas Eve for Mississauga to be with Dave, Sherri, and the kids. We had our traditional German-inspired Christmas Eve with a huge meal and then waddled to the living room to open gifts around the tree.

Mike did not join us from Montreal, but we called him later in the evening. The phone call didn't have much substance other than an exchange of Merry

Christmas wishes and thanks for gifts as the phone was passed around.

To my regret, he and I had lost touch during the years of my marriage, other than the odd birthday and Christmas cards or calls, but I called him when I separated, and we had a great chat. After that, we fell into the habit of chatting once a month or so.

My parents and Dave kept in touch with him, of course, but there was always a shroud over their conversations. Mike came home occasionally for visits, but he never brought Marc with him. In my conversations with Mike, I gleaned that they were a devoted couple and not prone to having multiple partners. We made plans for me to take the train to Montreal and I was looking forward to finally meeting Marc.

Most of us slept in on Christmas morning, excepting, of course for Dave and Sherri, who had a huge brunch waiting for us. After brunch, the kids went off to play with their new toys and Molson happily enjoyed his new bone while the rest of us sat around the table with coffee.

Dad took out his pipe and tobacco pouch and everyone sighed and rolled their eyes. He never actually smoked his pipe; it is more of a prop when he wants to talk about something. We had seen this a thousand times, so Sherri went to the kitchen and put on another pot of coffee as we all waited patiently.

"I'm thinking of retiring soon," he started, fiddling with his pipe. Mom had left her part-time job at the bank a few years before, but he had carried on with the consulting business. Mom was of the passbook and customer contact frame of mind and when ATMs came into play, she lost interest in the 'new processes,' as she called it. She had been after Dad to retire ever since then.

Their forever friends, the Hendersons, retired the previous year and rented a home in Florida that first winter. They liked it so much that they bought a home in a gated community in Fort Meyers and already left for their second winter there.

"Frank and Brenda have invited us to spend March with them in Florida, so we're going to see what all the fuss is about. I still have some clients to deal with but I'm thinking of spring as our target to wind things up."

"Do you think you might buy a place in Florida, Dad?" Dave asked.

"Let's not get ahead of ourselves; we haven't become Snowbirds just yet. We'll see what this trip to Florida brings."

"It would be nice to get away from the winter," I chimed in, as we all looked at the snow falling outside the window. "What would you do about the house, if you did decide to be away for six months of the year?"

"Baby steps," he replied. "Let's take this one step at a time."

We spent the next hour talking about their plans and then headed back to the city. It was snowing quite heavily, and we wanted to make the drive while it was still daylight. I was concerned about how my roommate had managed on his first night alone and had my fingers crossed that he hadn't wreaked havoc in my house.

As it turned out, there wasn't anything to worry about other than a single accidental or deliberate little gift on my bathroom floor. Zipper has a litter box, but he prefers the great outdoors. He made a beeline for the door when I got home, but came in shortly after, as it was snowing and cold. He did not let me off the hook, though, and while he enjoyed being warm and dry, he made his feelings clear by ignoring me for the rest of the night. I prepared his favourite meal which he ate like it might be his last. I noticed his curiosity as I unpacked my overnight bag and put my things away, but he quickly put his nose in the air when he caught me looking at him. He did join me in his special spot on the blanket box when I went to bed and the next morning, we were good friends again.

Chapter Five

THE BOX

MIKE AND I finally found a mutually convenient date for a visit to Montreal. Marc's weekends were busy at the restaurant and Mike was involved in a big project, but we agreed on the first week of March. I took a few days of holiday and decided to take the train for the fun of it. I left on a Monday morning, returning on Wednesday night. Ro and Joey agreed to look after Zipper while I was away.

I immediately fell in love with Montreal, their home, and Marc. Their loft was in an industrial building and has concrete floors and an exposed HVAC system and pipes, but they have filled it with colour. Besides being an amazing graphic artist, Mike was also a talented painter. He has a distinct style of painting faces abstractly. His work was different, but full of expression and colour. Many of his paintings hang in the loft and restaurant. I was particularly drawn to one painting that he said looked like me.

"Is that really how you see me?" I asked, tilting my head, and looking at the angles and bright colours. He laughed and presented it to me as a gift. I found another one that I knew Ro would like and insisted on buying it for her as a cat-sitting present.

Afterwards, they took me to see the sites all over Montreal and we had fabulous meals, both at the restaurant and at home. Marc was an amazing chef, and I ate to the point of explosion. We drank wine and talked far into the night, and I could see that they were not different from any couple who were devoted to each other. I was happy for them. I was also glad that I had my brother in my life again, along with his partner.

My parents came home from Florida at the end of the month energized and enthusiastic not only about the great weather, but the social life as well. They met a lot of Canadians in the community where the Hendersons live and confessed that they had made a conditional offer on a house there. Dad finished up the consulting work and by June they were ready to sell the house and start looking for a condo or apartment.

Dana knew a lot of Real Estate agents and she connected them with someone who delt with retirees wanting to downsize. The agent suggested they wait until they found what they wanted before listing the house in Leaside as she said it would sell fast.

It took almost three months, but they finally agreed on a condo they both liked in Etobicoke. They invited Dave and me to take whatever we wanted from the house.

They were getting some new furniture for the condo and selling or donating a lot of their old things. I picked a desk that Dad had used in the factory and later at home after the factory was sold. I moved it into my den and when I started to fill the drawers with my things, I found a ceramic shoe that I had given him as a gift when I was a young girl. That shoe had sat on this desk for many years, and I put it on the spot where Dad used to have it.

They moved into the condo in September and sold the house a few weeks later. They planned to leave for Florida at the beginning of November, after the closing date on the house. Dana drew up the paperwork and arranged for me to become their power of attorney if there were any issues. She also arranged for a cleaning company to come in and freshen up the house for the new owners.

With everything in place, we celebrated Thanksgiving, and off they went to their new life in retirement.

At the end of November, I got a phone call at the office from Adele, the real estate agent. I cringed, thinking something had gone terribly wrong, but she assured me it was nothing like that.

The house had four bedrooms on the second floor, one of which is very small, so my mother used it as a sewing room. The new owners decided to turn it into a walk-in closet to supplement the small closets in the other bedrooms. The existing closet in that room had a strange step up inside the door. My mother used the closet to store her sewing supplies and no one else ever ventured near it. A box was discovered inside that step up when the closet was demolished. They thought it was odd as it appeared to be hidden there but knowing my family had owned the house for many years, they felt it should be returned to us.

I told Adele I had no idea what the box was all about but asked if she would send it by messenger to my office.

It arrived in a packing box and when I opened it the next evening, I found what appeared to be either a large jewelry box or a small hope chest inside. Turning it around, I noticed two small brass hinges on the back and a latch with a brass lock on the front. I pictured a small key but had no idea where such a key would be found.

Zipper jumped up on the chair to examine the box and gave me an inquiring look.

"I have no idea what this is, Zipper, but it is very strange."

My first thought was to call my parents in Florida, but they had left on a cruise to the Caribbean with Frank and Brenda and a few others to celebrate their retirement.

I was undecided about what to do, but my parents had given me their power of attorney, so I did have the right to act on their behalf. Still, I hesitated as the box was locked and someone had taken pains to keep it hidden.

Zipper sniffed at the box and meowed.

"Yes, I'm curious, too but you have nine lives, Zipper. There could be anything in that box."

Giving in to temptation, using a small pair of pliers, I snapped the lock off the latch and held my breath as I carefully opened the lid. The box was filled with several letters tied with ribbon, addressed to my grandmother, with a return address of someone I did not know from a place called Wernigerode in Germany.

Frowning, I carefully set the packet of letters aside without undoing the ribbon and peered back into the box. There were three notebooks. I opened one. It was written in German, so I could not read it, but the date was 1913.

As I moved the notebooks, I spotted a small velvet bag. I picked it up and pulled the attached string. A gold wedding band popped out and spun across the table. I stepped back and put my hand over my thumping heart as I watched the ring come to a stop on the table.

I looked around the dining room as if someone would magically materialize and explain this to me, but there was no one there.

I slowly picked up the gold ring, put it back in the velvet bag, returned it, the letters, and the notebook to the box, and closed the lid.

I was spending Christmas at home this year which suited me fine. There were a lot of things going on in the month of December, starting with a trip to the tree farm with Ro and Joey to pick out a live tree for my living room. I had been looking forward to it all week, but I could not shake my mood. I hadn't slept well the past few nights thinking about the box.

Joey scampered ahead in search of the perfect tree as soon as he got out of the car. It was a dull, overcast morning and a chilly wind blew around the trees. I crossed my arms in front of me and burrowed deeper into my coat for warmth.

The tree guy offered coffee, bless him, so Ro and I indulged as we wandered around. Before long Joey called out that he had made a few choices and we headed in his direction. We debated his choices and decided on one that we all agreed would be perfect. I paid the tree guy, and he stuffed the tree as far as he could into my hatchback. Ro and I gave Joey a high five, then headed home. Back at home the three of us wrestled the tree out of the trunk and laid it on the front porch to wait until the next weekend.

I made comfort food, consisting of hot soup and grilled cheese sandwiches which warmed us up quickly. Ro had brought supplies for Joey to make a looped paper garland for the tree. We settled him at the table with red and green paper, scissors, and a stapler while I made tea.

We sat in the living room, me on the sofa and Ro in the armchair across from me with her feet up on the ottoman.

"All right, spill it, girl," she said as she sipped her tea. "What's wrong with you today?"

I sighed as I sat back on the sofa, cradling my cup with both hands, and told her about the call from Adele, the delivery of the box to my office, and the step-up in the closet. She said she had heard about those closets and thought the step was there for women to stand on to reach hat boxes on the shelf.

I confessed that I broke the lock and opened the box.

I told Ro about the contents of the box, and we talked about it until Joey called out that he was done. He made a few perfectly imperfect garlands, and I gave him a big squeeze. Ro cleared away the art supplies while I found a cookie for him and a treat for Zipper. We settled

Joey in the corner of the sofa with a book, but within minutes his eyes got heavy, and he was asleep. I covered him with an Afghan from the back of the sofa as Ro asked to see the box.

I lifted the box from on top of the pie cupboard in the dining room and placed it on the ottoman as she and I sat cross-legged on the floor. She looked to me for reassurance before opening it. I nodded, affirmatively. The first thing she took out was the velvet bag and looked at the gold ring inside. She turned it around in her hand and held it up to see if there was an inscription inside. Not finding one she gently placed it back in the bag. Then she took out one of the hardcover notebooks and paged through it. The writing was on both sides of the page and every inch was covered in that slant typical of Europeans.

"Boy, they didn't waste anything in those days, did they?" she remarked.

"Especially paper," I responded.

"These are journals," she said softly. She looked at the packet of letters and the name in the upper left corner. "Who is Greta Baehr?" she asked.

Shrugging I answered, "I have no idea."

"You've never heard that name before?" I shook my head. "What about the address in *Wernigerode?*"

I went into the den and got the atlas off the bookshelf. We opened it to the page containing Germany and found Wernigerode in small letters near *Hamburg* on the North Sea.

"Your grandmother's name was Ava Langner," she observed. That was her married name. We both thought about the elephant in the room or the velvet bag in this case. My grandmother had worn a wedding ring, but not this one.

"Would your parents or your father at least know anything about this? Or could he translate the journals and letters?" Ro asked as she sat back against the chair.

"My first instinct was to call him in Florida, but they are away on a cruise. Now that I know what's in the box, I'm not sure what to do. My grandmother obviously had taken great pains to keep it hidden," I added.

"Do you think your father knows Greta Baehr?"

"I'll be talking to them and the boys over Christmas, but I think this is a conversation best held in person. They won't be back until spring. You're the only person I've talked to about this."

Ro gave me a sidelong glance and said, "What do you know about your grandmother's past?"

I considered what little I knew. My grandparents had emigrated from Germany, and as far as I knew had always lived in that house. My father could speak and understand some German, but I doubted he was proficient at it having gone to school here.

"What are you going to do about this?" Ro asked me.

"I don't know," I replied standing and picking up the box. She gave me another measured look. "That box was locked and well hidden. Obviously, my parents didn't know it was there or they would have taken it with them when they sold the house. Who knows what's in those journals and letters"?

Joey was waking up on the sofa and Ro glanced out the window as she went to pick him up. It was late afternoon by now and getting dark.

"It's still snowing," she said. "I should get this guy home."

Chapter Six

LORNA

THE FOLLOWING SATURDAY afternoon I was busy giving the house a good cleaning and preparing a large tray of lasagna for the party. I had purchased some lights and decorations for the tree, which were in a box on the coffee table.

The guys brought the tree in from the front porch, and we decided it would be best beside the sofa where it would be seen from outside.

They set it up in the stand and strung the lights around in an even pattern. Dean built a fire in the fireplace.

"The manly stuff is done," John said, flexing his muscles while he switched on the tree lights. "Now we party." He and Dean retreated to the dining room to attack the appetizers and beer.

I poured wine for the girls; we grabbed a few treats and set about decorating the tree. I grabbed the box of ornaments. The girls all brought an ornament of their own, and Joey's perfectly imperfect garlands were the final touch.

We stood back to admire our work and agreed that Joey's garlands took the decorations to the next level. "He really is the most amazing creature on God's green earth," I said laughing.

"The lasagna smells delicious," said Linda as she headed to the kitchen.

"Will you put the garlic bread in the oven, please," I called out as I gathered up the empty boxes.

We sat around the dining room table, eating, drinking, and laughing. Just a group of thirty-somethings enjoying each other's company. Later Dana suggested a walk.

"I'm so full I need to walk some of this off before I burst!"

We bundled up and headed to the nearby park. The lights sparkled in the cold clear night and a half-moon shone over the lake. We admired the lights on houses along the way back and declared the tree in my front window a success.

"Irish coffee," said Dean, rubbing his hands. We made coffee and Dean fixed the drinks with a flair. We sat around the living room and began talking as the evening started to wind down.

"Don't forget our open house on Boxing Day," Dana called out as they were leaving.

"I'm bartender," said John, bowing at the waist and putting an imaginary towel across his arm. "So, the drinks will be fabulous."

Ro offered to help clean up, as Joey was with Tom and she was in no hurry to get home. We made a half-hearted effort but then collapsed in the living room.

"I'm exhausted," she said. The run-up to Christmas had her kids bouncing off walls at school. "And all the booze I've consumed tonight, yikes."

Zipper had been outside all evening, but I could hear him at the patio door. He strolled in and stopped dead when he saw the tree.

"Just hope he doesn't decide to climb it," Ro said with a laugh. "Have you given any more thought to what you'll do about the box?"

"It's all I think about, but I need a translator and I am just not sure how to go about it. There could be sensitive stuff in those letters and journals."

"Have you decided not to talk to your father about it?"

I shrugged. "I'm really undecided about it. I should just turn it over to him, but what if there are things that he doesn't know about? He did not have the best relationship with my grandfather, and I don't want to upset him. My parents have never been big on sharing that kind of thing. They think if they don't talk about something it doesn't exist."

"Katie's mother Lorna is a retired teacher. She has been giving us a hand at school this year. We think she is lonely since Katie's father passed away and it gives her something to do. We are glad for her help, believe me, especially at this time of the year.

Anyway, she grew up in Germany. She met Katie's father when he was with the Canadian Armed Forces, in England, I think. I'm not sure how she ended up in England, but at any rate, they got married there and she returned with him. She may be the ideal person to translate for you."

"I'm not sure, Ro. I'm dying to know what is written in there but am anxious about it at the same time."

"Maybe it's serendipitous that it came into your hands. If your parents had found the box when they moved or anytime over the years, they lived in that house your father may have been able to understand enough of it to keep it underground forever."

"And that is what has been keeping me up nights." I sighed. "At least I have you to talk to about it."

"Being co-conspirator appeals to my sense of adventure." She winked at me. "Anyway, Lorna is a lovely woman and does not appear to be the gossipy type. I'll mention it to her if you like."

I agreed but asked Ro to just tell Lorna that I had some documents that needed translating and not get into the whole story.

Ro groaned as she stood up. "Geez, Sar, I'll be glad when school is out next week. Great party, by the way, and your tree is awesome."

She hugged me as she struggled into her coat. "Don't wait too long to decide— the suspense is killing me."

The Christmas season flew by with lots of activities, both at the office and on the Beaches. Everyone was busy on New Year's Eve, but I was happy to spend it at home with Zipper. Ro met someone new, at the supermarket of all places. She is careful about whom she dates and never brings anyone home to meet Joey. But she said this guy was different and after a few coffee and lunch dates he invited her to a dinner and dance for New Year's Eve. Joey was with Tom, so she got dressed up for her first New Year's Eve party in years.

It was now the first Saturday in January, and I was at Dad's desk paying bills and sorting through junk mail that had landed there over the holidays. I came across a piece of paper with Lorna's phone number that Ro had left there. Even though I had been busy the past few weeks, the box was always in the back of my mind. I talked to my parents and the boys over the holidays but didn't feel it was the time to mention it.

I turned the paper over in my hand and decided it was now or never, I dialed Lorna's number and introduced myself when she picked up.

"Oh, yes, you are Rosemary's friend. She told me about you."

We chatted amicably about the Christmas season and the weather and then I got to it. "I'm not sure if Ro told you, but I am looking for someone who may be able to translate some documents written in German."

"Well, I am bilingual, but by no means a trained translator. Are these documents of a legal or professional nature?"

"No, no, nothing like that. It is more of an ancestral type of thing."

"I would be happy to help you if I can. When did you want to do this?"

"This information came into my hands several weeks ago, but I've been too busy to do anything about it." I hesitated but said, "But now that the holiday rush is over, I would like to explore it as soon as possible. Would you meet me for coffee, perhaps, and we could discuss it further?"

"Sure, that would be fine."

"Is tomorrow too soon?" I laughed. "I'm sorry. When would be convenient for you?"

She laughed too and said that tomorrow would suit her fine. She told me she goes to church at eleven but could meet me at twelve-thirty, so we agreed on a café not far from her church.

I decided to go to the shopping center and picked up envelopes on my way. I stopped at the electronics store and bought a small tape recorder and a package of cassettes.

I arrived early at the café the next day and chose a table by the window. A car parked a few minutes later and I watched as a woman got out and crossed the parking lot. She was wearing a beautifully tailored camel coat with killer black boots. Confession, I am a shoe girl, probably due to my heritage.

She noticed me and smiled as soon as she walked in. She hung her coat on the hall tree and walked toward me removing her leather gloves.

I stood up and she said, "You must be Sarah. I'm Lorna."

We ordered tea and I said, "Would you like to have lunch? I'm sure you haven't eaten as you just came from church."

"Yes, that would be nice."

There were no menus on the table but a blackboard on the wall listed the choices. When the waiter brought our pot of tea along with two fancy mugs, we both ordered quiche and salad.

"This is definitely a ladies' café," I said, appreciating the service and the environment.

"Yes, I come here with a friend from church sometimes and they will keep filling the teapot as often as you like." She smiled and I had to agree with Ro that she was, indeed, a lovely lady.

We chatted over lunch. She told me that she and her husband, Frank had made great plans for their retirement. They sold their house and moved into an apartment so they could just lock the door and travel. Sadly, he passed away before they got that far. But she keeps busy with friends, her church, and volunteer work. Katie, her daughter, and Katie's husband Ian are close, but her son is living in Vancouver, so she doesn't see him very often. She is hoping that Katie and Ian will make her a grandmother sometime soon.

Conversation lagged for a minute until I said, "My mother would love that scarf you're wearing."

She smiled, "I have a drawer full of scarves and love them all. I've been getting them as gifts for years, so it has become my signature thing."

"My mother, too."

The waiter came by to remove our dishes and refill the teapot. I opened my oversized handbag and brought out the journal.

"Lorna, I believe this journal was written by my grandmother. It has just surfaced recently, and I would really like to know what she wrote about."

I handed it across the table to her and she reached into her bag for her glasses.

"What year was your grandmother born?"

"I believe she was born in 1897."

"It says 1913, so she would have only been 16 when she wrote this." She studied the first few pages and said, "Your grandmother must have been an educated woman for her day, Sarah, as this appears to be well written. And her handwriting is impeccable. My parents were just a few years older than her, but neither of them could write this well. Where did she grow up?"

"As far as I know in *Wernigerode*, near *Hamburg*."

"Ah, in Northern Germany. My family is from a small village called Seligenstadt in the Black Forest area."

She noticed my frown and raised her eyebrows in question.

"My grandmother died when I was young, and I know so little about her. My father never talked about her much," I explained.

"Are you concerned about what may be in this journal?"

"Yes, yes, I am, to be honest with you." I did not want to go into the details of the 'box' just yet, and she did not ask me how or why my grandmother's past was suddenly important to me. I appreciated her discretion, which heightened my trust in her.

"This was written just before the war. Many, many things happened through those years that people simply did not talk about. It was a terrible time in Europe and did not end when the war was over. Spanish flu came next, which wiped out millions of people. My family lost a lot, as did many others. It is a wonder they survived at all. I was born in 1922 when things were just starting to improve, but it was a hard life for my parents. I'm sure there is a lot I never knew about them."

She paged through the journal a bit more and I could see she was interested but somewhat troubled.

"Sarah, I would like to delve into this, but only if you agree. How would it be if I take it home with me and see how it goes? If you are unhappy with the contents, we can stop any time."

I reached back into my bag and pulled out the tape recorder and cassettes. "I brought this just in case you decided to get involved. I thought it would be easier for you to read into the tape recorder rather than having to write anything out."

She smiled. "Thank you. That was thoughtful of you."

The waiter came by with our check and Lorna reached for her purse. "No, please, let me," I said.

We were both pensive as we walked out to the parking lot.

"I hope I haven't reminded you of your own family's history, Lorna."

She smiled and patted the journal that she held against her. Impulsively I reached out to hug her, and she embraced me in return. I gave her my phone number and she said she would call me.

Chapter Seven

1913

I HAVE LIVED IN this house for three years now. I came to replace my sister Greta when I was thirteen. Greta also came when she was thirteen, but at sixteen she was called home to marry a man of our father's choosing.

Her duties were mostly as a nanny to the two young children of Herr Koenig and his wife. Christian and Julia were older by the time I arrived, and now attend a private school for part of each day, so my duties also include helping in the kitchen and serving in the dining room.

The Koenig family is very wealthy, and their home is beautiful. My home in Wernigerode is a fraction in size and holds none of the fineries of this house. The cook, Frau Ursula, (or Cook as she is called), does not live in the house but arrives promptly at 7:00 am to light the fire in the stove and begin preparations for the day. I sleep in a tiny room off the kitchen and rise early to help her. We prepare breakfast for the children; I help them dress and walk them to school each morning.

Herr Koenig owns a shipping business and has many ships in his fleet. They are constantly coming or going from the harbour. He fills them with equipment, machinery, and items built in Hamburg and they return with fabric, spices, and other things from far away.

When he is home there are many dinner parties as he is a very prominent man. Cook spends all day preparing and will often yell at me to do this or that. I know she wants everything to be perfect for the Koenigs and their guests. We feed Christian and Julia, the Koenig children, in the kitchen and I prepare them for bed before changing into a crisp uniform to serve in the dining room.

I am a servant and invisible, but I enjoy these dinner parties. I hear of things that I do not understand but I like to study their splendid clothing and manners. When I have cleared away the dishes and served coffee, Cook and I will do the washing up. She is always weary as she leaves out the back door.

Herr Koenig is often away on one of his ships, sometimes for weeks at a time. He goes to England often but has made long voyages to America. The stories of these trips told around the dining room table are fascinating.

When he is gone, Frau Koenig spends more time with her lady friends. They meet in the parlour where I serve tea and pastries. My work is lighter, so I spend more time with the children when they return from school.

One day she noticed me trying to follow along in their books as we sat at the kitchen table.

"My goodness, Ava, are you trying to read?"

I blush up to my hair line and Cook gives me a measured look from her place at the stove.

"She is like a sponge, Mama," Julia said. "She learns faster than some of the students at school."

Frau Koenig frowns but does not say any more. What she does not know is that Julia and Christian also let me watch when they practice the piano and sometimes will allow me to touch the keys.

I am happy in this house and living in Hamburg, but it is 1913 and I am approaching my sixteenth birthday. I am praying that my father is not looking for a husband for me. I have only been home once to visit my family in the past year.

Greta is nineteen now. She lives in a row house with her husband, a two-year-old son, and is expecting another child. There are many Baehr families in our community and the man our father chose for her is also a Baehr. He is probably a second cousin to us.

We sit in her small garden shelling peas, and I chatter on about learning to read, write, and play the piano, but she shakes her head at me.

"Who do you think you are, Avie? Girls like us have no need for those things. You better not let Papa hear you."

I speak no more about it. Greta can read and write, but my knowledge is better.

She and I are like many German girls from small villages. We are put into servitude at a young age and see a different life in the city but usually end up with the same life our parents have known. Many are married off as young as fourteen if a placement cannot be found, and we know girls who have three or more children by the time they are Greta's age.

She stops shelling peas and we both look down the long row of houses along the road. She sighs but says nothing. I wonder if she is happy in this life, which is so much like the lives of those who came before us, but I will not ask.

Boys stay home and help the family. Many go to work on the farms and some, like my father, rarely leave the area. He may go to the city with the wagon to deliver vegetables to the market but that is about as far as he has ever travelled. In this way, the girls often know more about the world beyond our small village than the boys do. I look at Greta again and feel guilty that I do not want her life.

We have two older siblings, both boys. I am the youngest so there is no one to take my place in the Koenig household. My father says nothing to me on this visit, so either he has not found a suitable candidate for me to marry, or he is happy for me to stay where I am. My earnings are sent to him every three months, so I am doing my part to help the family.

The year turned to 1914 and things are changing in the Koenig household. Herr Koenig is home more but his ships seem to be sailing more often from the harbour. There are many dinner parties and I often hear the word politics, as I go about my job of serving. I ask Cook what 'politics' means but she does not know. She is exhausted more often these days with all the people in the house and short-tempered, too.

The men will stay at the dining room table after dinner now with brandy and cigars while the women retreat to the parlour where they pick up sewing and gossip. Many times, I hear the men's voices raised through the door as Cook and I clean up, but I do not know what they are saying. The word war is mentioned more and more which has a bad sound to it.

I go about my work unnoticed, so no one sees some of the things I do. I will sneak one of the children's books and read it in my small room at night with the door open. No one comes to the kitchen, so they do not see my oil lamp burning. I am sure I would be in trouble if Herr Koenig knew what I was doing.

One of the families that come to the house often is the Meyers. Herr Meyer owns a factory that produces wallpaper. All the best families, including the Koenig's, have wallpaper on their walls in flocked patterns on heavy paper or cloth.

The Meyer family has two sons; Hans is twenty-two and Rauf a few years younger. Hans is serious and will sit with the older men, sometimes joining in their conversations. But Rauf is fun-loving and playful. He is good-looking and winked at me once when he caught me staring at him. After that, he would sometimes come into the kitchen to tease Cook and me while we go about our work. She tries to shoo him out, but he just laughs.

Hans scolds Rauf many times for not taking things more seriously, but Rauf just shrugs it off. He starts to pay attention, however, when he learns that his father is planning to retool the factory to prepare for the war effort. Hans joined the army, but Rauf has no interest in doing that. He is shocked to learn that all young men may be forced to do so soon.

Rauf started to visit the Koenig house on his own more often. He left me a note in the kitchen one day to meet him in the garden. I slipped away as soon as I could and joined him on a bench behind some large bushes that blocked us from the view of the house. We talked about a lot of things and after that, I would meet him there as often as I could. He told me he designed some of the wallpaper patterns and it is his ambition to become a great designer one day. I have never known anyone with ambition—it is exciting, and I am drawn to him.

I have no way of knowing what a relationship between a man and a woman should be like, but from the whispers I hear from Greta and other married girls, it is something that men enjoy, and women endure. Rauf kissed me one day in the garden and I felt it to the tips of my fingers and toes. I thought I could endure this very well. But I would not tell anyone I felt that way.

The idea of the son of a wealthy prominent family and a servant girl was too farfetched to even think about. Yet I found myself daring to believe that such a thing could be possible, and my dreams are of Rauf.

Rauf tells me he wants to go to America. He knows his father will never approve but he hates the thought of war and believes America is free of such oppression. He asks me to go with him, which makes my heart thump, but I am horrified by the thought. He tells me that he loves me, and I know I love him, but the idea is so outrageous that I cannot even consider it.

I know he will leave when he gets the chance and I am frightened because we are doing things I know are wrong, but I cannot help myself. I was raised to be a quiet girl, to do as I am told, and certainly not to question the traditions of my family or my place in life. But the power of love has me in its hold, and instinctively I know I will never feel this way about another man. It has also crossed my mind that another man will not want me when they find out the things I have done with Rauf, but the thought of another man touching me makes me shudder. I know I would be judged harshly for my behaviour, as I should be, but how could such a beautiful thing be so bad?

In June, Herr Koenig is given an appointment by the government. There is concern that Great Britain is about to enter the Allied Powers and fight against Germany. His ships are sent off to England in haste to acquire textiles and woollens to make uniforms. Rauf volunteers to go to England with the fleet of ships on this mission. He tells me he plans to go to America from England and tries again to convince me to go with him, but I cannot.

Able-bodied men are conscripted into the army and women are hustled into factories to make ammunition and uniforms. I escape the factory as I am needed in the Koenig household. There are endless meetings and gatherings during this prewar period and Cook and I spend many hours in the kitchen.

Herr Koenig's ships return in good time from England loaded down with raw materials, but Rauf does not return. Frau Koenig is trying to console Frau Meyer, but the men are furious. They are yelling at each other in the dining room and my hands shake as I serve coffee. No one notices me. I am heartbroken and more frightened than ever, but too afraid to tell anyone of his plans.

On July 28, 1914, war erupted in Europe. The world has turned upside down and us with it. Everyone is afraid, including me, but I have a much more personal reason. I suspect that I am pregnant.

The tape ended with a click and Lorna's voice faded into the room. For a moment no one said anything.

When Lorna invited me to her apartment to listen to the tape, I asked if Ro could join us, largely because I was nervous and apprehensive.

Lorna broke the silence by standing and gathering our cups and moving into the kitchen. She returned with a bottle of wine and three glasses as Ro was asking, "Isn't your father's name Rauf?"

"Yes, but he was born in May of 1918 and my grandfather was named William. Does this mean my grandmother had another baby, four years earlier in Hamburg? How did she end up in Canada married to William and what happened to that baby? As far as I know, my father was an only child."

Lorna poured the wine and said, "Good questions, Sarah."

Ro nudged me with her foot under the table.

I cleared my throat. "Full disclosure, Lorna. When my grandparents died in the '60s my family moved into their home in Leaside. My parents lived there until last year when they downsized, bought a condo in Etobicoke and a home in Florida. The Box was found by the new owners when they renovated one of the bedrooms and it was given to me. There are two other journals and some letters in the Box."

"Now we know that Greta was your grandmother's sister, and the letters were from her. Wernigerode was their home," Ro said.

"Do your parents know about the box?" Lorna asked.

"Well, no. I'm sure they didn't know it was there. It came into my hands when they were on a cruise, and

I couldn't reach them. It was locked and I confess that I broke into it out of curiosity. It's a long story, but my father never talked about his parent's past, so I have no idea if he knows any of this."

"Hmm, so if there are more journals and letters, we may be able to continue the story. Is that what you want to do?"

I reached into my bag and pulled out the second journal and a new cassette.

"Yes, I do."

Chapter Eight

RO AND BEN

IN EARLY FEBRUARY Lorna called one evening as I was pushing the vacuum cleaner around. We chatted for a bit, and she told me she had translated the second journal. On impulse, I invited her for dinner. She accepted and said she would bring the journal and tape. We made a date for the following Sunday. I invited Ro as well.

Ro said she had to be home by 8:00. She wanted to make sure she was there when Joey got home from his dad's. I had told Lorna 4:00 o'clock so that worked well.

She mentioned that she had a date with Ben on Saturday night. "When are we going to meet him," I asked, and we both laughed.

The previous Friday night the gang had met at *Frogs*. Katie and Ian joined us and someone asked Ro when we were going to meet her supermarket find.

"I'll bet he wears a hairnet and works at the deli counter," said John. Ro threw a piece of bread stick at him and said "I met him at the supermarket, he doesn't work there, you dolt. He's an engineer." Several pairs of eyebrows went up as the girls looked at each other.

"Oh, he's not a mere mortal like the rest of us" sighed John. "Well, you won't see *him* on the next firemen`s calendar, will you?" said Dean flexing an arm muscle. Ro said he would put both the guys to shame. Ian is a banker and he preened a bit too so Ro threw the rest of her bread stick at him.

"From what I can tell, he is quite attractive," said Dana, sipping her wine with a knowing look.

"Are you spying on me?" Said Ro.

"Of course, I'm the Neighbourhood Watch, don't you know."

"More like the neighbourhood busy body," said John. "But you should bring him around so we can all gawk at him." Ro just rolled her eyes and dug into the food on the table.

We were having a thaw and it was pouring rain on Sunday, making the snow into a slushy mess. Lorna arrived, with the hood on her jacket up over her hair and drops of rain dripping from her shoulders. She set her purse, a canvas tote bag, and a bottle of wine down and removed her boots. I took her coat to hang in the bathroom to dry.

I directed her to the living room after giving her a full tour of the place. I had a fire burning, and a few candles lit on the mantel. The room was cozy and warm.

"It's lovely, Sarah, so charming."

Ro came in the side door. "Sarah, it smells divine in here. I've been doing prep work for my class all afternoon and I'm starving."

Zipper came out of hiding when he heard Ro's voice.

"This is the infamous Zipper?" Lorna asked. "May I pick him up?"

He looked her over carefully, decided she looked good, and settled in for some cuddles.

I prepared a beef roast, with the veggies in the same pan, so that I wouldn't have to spend time in the kitchen.

We settled around the table and over dinner Lorna told us she had just returned from St. Catharines. "I was visiting my sister-in-law for a few days and came straight from there this afternoon."

She told us that Margery is Frank's sister and the two couples had been good friends. Margery lost her husband, John, a few years before Frank died. She sold her house and moved to St. Catharines to be close to her grandchildren. She and Margery stayed in contact and visited as often as possible.

"We went to Niagara Falls, New York, over the river as they say to do some shopping at the outlet malls and met friends of Margery's for dinner. Margery is going to Arizona with them for six weeks and they invited me along."

"You should go" Ro and I both said.

"I'm thinking about it. They are driving but I would fly and just stay for a week or so. They are friends of Marg's, and it was nice of them to ask but I wouldn't want to overstay my welcome."

After dinner, Ro and I cleared the table and brought out dessert.

"Tea or wine?"

We decided on wine as there was still some on the table. Lorna had picked up the canvas bag and removed the tape, journal, and her own notebook. Here we go, I thought.

There was a slight pause again, then my grandmother spoke through Lorna's voice.

Chapter Nine

ERIK

IT BECAME CLEAR by autumn of last year that I am indeed pregnant. I was sick for many weeks in the morning, but if I ate a bit of bread, I usually felt better by the time Cook arrived. Gradually this went away, but the cigar smoke in the dining room bothers me sometimes. I run to the garden to throw up. Cook sees but says nothing. No one else notices me as I run back and forth constantly while serving.

The Koenig house has many people most days and everyone is so busy. The dining room table is full of maps and charts that Herr Koenig and the men are always studying. Frau Koenig is in the parlour with the women cutting long strips of fabric to roll into bandages or knitting socks and hats. Christian and Julia feel the strain, too. They have a private tutor now and disappear to the second floor. We no longer spend our days reading books or playing the piano.

One morning Cook asks me to take a cup of tea to Frau Koenig in the parlour. She is alone and sitting on the settee with her head down reading. I am very worried as my uniform is stretched tight and I am afraid the seams will burst. I wear my apron up high around my chest, but it no longer hides the roundness of my body. As I bend to put the teacup on the table a strange sensation goes through me. I gasp and both hands go to my belly.

Frau Koenig looks up.

"Ava," she says frowning. I collapse into tears, and they just keep flowing as I lean forward. I am afraid the baby is going to burst right out of me.

She takes my hand and sits me beside her on the settee.

"Ava," she said again and put her hand on my belly. The sensation came again, and she sat back with a start.

"Are you ...? It can't be." Her face is filled with horror. "How did this happen?"

She is shaken but then her face turns to rage. "Did someone violate you?"

I look at her with tears streaming down my face and realize she is thinking that one of the men who come to the house has done this to me.

I did not want her to think that, but I am afraid to speak of Rauf. Most of all I was afraid of what will happen to me and my unborn baby.

"Please don't send me away like that other girl."

"What other girl?" she asks sharply. She notices Cook frowning at the doorway and tells her to go back to the kitchen. "This doesn't concern you."

Cook gives me a nasty look, but turns and walks away.

Cook takes me to the butcher shop sometimes if she has a lot of packages to carry. I overheard her talking to another cook about a maid that works in the home where she is employed. That girl was sent away, and her baby was placed in an orphanage. No one knows what happened to the girl, but she never returned.

I told Frau Koenig this and she shook her head. "I know about that, but I don't agree. You are my responsibility, just as that girl was the responsibility of her mistress. She was thinking about protecting herself and her husband from gossip." She frowned, and I knew she was thinking of her own household.

She was quiet for a moment, then picked up her tea and offered it to me. I take a sip, but it is difficult to swallow.

"You must tell me who did this to you."

I hung my head in shame and started to sob again. It took all my courage to whisper, "Rauf."

"Rauf? Rauf Meyer did this? That useless insolent scoundrel." She stood and paced the room. "No one even knows where he is." She is wringing her hands but sees that I am near hysterics. She sits down beside me and puts her arm around me. "I'd like to throttle that boy," she mutters as she rocks me gently.

I confess that we are in love.

"In love!" She puts her hand under my chin giving me no choice but to look up into her eyes.

"How could he leave knowing that you are pregnant?"

"No, no, he did not know about it when he left."

"Did he ask you to go with him?"

"Yes, but I could not dare to do such a thing."

"Do you know where Rauf is?" she asks after a few moments.

"No, but he told me he wanted to go to America."

"America!" she says softly. "Ava you must not speak of this to anyone."

Things changed after that. I got a new uniform and Cook is more cross with me than ever. A midwife came to see me and said I would have the baby before the end of the year. I am glad that I work for Frau Koenig instead of that other lady, but I am still terrified. It does not appear that she has told Herr Koenig of my condition, but I do not know how much longer before my secret is out. My feet and legs are swollen and I am tired all the time, but I continue with my duties.

The wives do not come as often in December. They are preparing for Christmas in their households, in whatever form it may take this year. Cook and I only have the men to contend with which is a blessing for us both.

I am helping her prepare the evening meal when I am suddenly struck by pain so strong that it almost knocks me to the floor. Then I feel a wetness running down my legs and puddling on the floor. Cook runs for Frau Koenig in the parlour. She yells at Cook to go for the midwife after she goes to the garden shed for a tarp. She spreads the tarp on my bed with a blanket on top and tells me to lie down. The pains are coming every few minutes now and I curl into a ball, holding my stomach, trying not to scream.

The midwife asks Frau Koenig for some towels and water. She ties one of the towels to the bedpost and tells me to hold the other end when the pain comes. They closed the door to my room. The air is hot and dry. The midwife baths my face and hands with cool water, but it is hard to breathe. As the night wears on, she opens the door to the kitchen. There is no one there, so she is not so concerned that someone will see what is happening. The fresher air from the kitchen feels so much better and I am a bit more relaxed.

I hear Cook arrive and the midwife telling her that it should not be much longer. She asks for hot water and clean towels. I am so tired, but she tells me to push again. I do not think I have the strength, but I begin to push and suddenly I feel emptiness, and my baby is gone from my body. The midwife calls for Cook to take the baby while she massages my stomach. I feel another voiding, then fall back against the bed. I hear the midwife telling Cook the baby is small and not too much damage has been done, but I feel as though my body has been ravaged.

I am not sure how much time passes before the midwife places my baby boy on my chest. He is small and his cries sound like those of a small kitten. The house is awakening, and Frau Koenig comes into the room and closes the door.

The midwife is writing something on a piece of paper.

"What is your name?" she asks, "and the father's name?"

Frau Koenig and I look at each other and I say, "My name is Ava Baehr, and he will be called Erik Baehr."

She does not ask any questions as she writes this on the paper. Frau Koenig reaches into her pocket and gives the midwife some coins. She cleans up after herself and is gone.

Frau Koenig sets the paper on the little table beside my bed and leaves the room. Sometime later I look at the paper and it simply reads:

A son was born to Ava Baehr on December 15, 1914. He is named Erik Baehr.

Chapter Ten

YOUNG GIRLS

ERIK IS SEVEN months old now. He lives with me in my little room off the kitchen and I tend to him between my other duties. I breastfeed him, but sometimes he must wait. He is still so small and does not fuss. He sleeps in a little basket during the day, but at night I hold him in my bed and try to comfort him. I talk and sing to him, but there are nights when I am so tired that I cry because I think he needs so much more.

The fighting across Europe continues and the household is busier than ever. Sometimes Frau Koenig will take me to the hospital with her. Injured men are returning now, and she takes bandages to them and helps tend to the wounded where she can. I am shocked by what has happened to these men and notice that some of them appear to be in a dazed state. I hear the nurses talking about something called 'shell shock.' One day, Frau Koenig crosses herself in the carriage on the way home and tells me they are so glad that their son Christian is too young to be sent to the army.

I fashion a sling that I tie around my neck and waist so that I can carry Erik with me when I run errands. He does not weigh much, but some days the load is heavy if I have several parcels to carry, but he needs to get out of the house and into the fresh air. One day I meet some women from Wernigerode at the market. They are unloading a wagon of vegetables. They tell me that food is scarce at home because a lot of produce from the farms is needed in the city. It is clear that this is a burden to them in many ways.

I ask about my family and their faces are distraught. They tell me that word has come that my eldest brother has died and the whereabouts of my other brother are unknown. My father has taken this news very badly and can no longer do much. My parents have moved into Greta's home which has made things difficult for her. I have almost forgotten about Erik in my distress, but he pokes his head out of the sling. The women are shocked to see him, and I must confess that he is my son. They exchange looks of surprise. I cry as I walk home, for my family, and many other families that have had losses. I hold my son close but know that these women will tell my family about him, which will cause them more distress.

The months drag on and another Christmas passes. Erick has his first birthday, but no one noticed. He spends more time in the kitchen now, but he is startled by every noise and hides behind a cupboard if anyone comes by. I am careful to keep him out of Cook's way.

One of my duties is to collect the mail from the post office. The government censors the mail now, but Herr

Koenig is an important man, and his mail is not blocked. The Postmaster hands me a packet of letters tied with string. I always hope there may be a letter from Greta, so I look through the packet. I almost faint in the street when I see a small blue envelope addressed to me with Air Mail written on the front. I stick it deep in my apron pocket and run home as fast as I can. I am busy all day, but my heart is pounding as I touch my apron several times to make sure it is still there.

Late at night, I open this letter in my room. Rauf! The letter is dated many weeks before. My hands are shaking as I read that he is living in Jersey City, New Jersey, USA. He works in a textile factory and has approached the owner with some of his designs. He has made some friends and lives with another German man named William, in what he calls a flat.

He sailed to America from England as a working crew member almost a year and a half ago. He misses his family but has been afraid to write as he knows they are disappointed in him. But he says he misses me more and wishes I could join him in America. Nothing is happening there yet, but there is talk of war. He is hoping this letter will not fall into the hands of someone other than me. He says if I do receive it, to write back to him in secret if possible.

Erik mutters in his sleep. I am good at keeping secrets, I whisper as I tuck in his blanket and watch him settle back into sleep.

I carry Rauf's letter with me for days while my heart aches for him. I write to him and tell him everything. He has the right to know that he is a father and that I miss him, too.

The tape clicked off and silence took the place of Lorna's voice for a few moments.

"That poor girl," said Ro. "I can't imagine giving birth like that. Joey was born in a clean sterile hospital with me screaming for drugs. And her baby—imagine having to keep that kind of a secret." Ro had tears in her eyes.

"It's a wonder more women didn't die in childbirth in those times," said Lorna.

Ro looked at her watch. "Yikes, speaking of children, I've got to run. Joey will be home soon."

"Go ahead, dear, I'll help Sarah clean up."

We were quiet as we cleared the dessert dishes and glasses from the table.

Lorna looked pensive as we moved into the living room for tea. "Are you sure you want to continue with this, Sarah?"

"Yes, I need to know. I still don't understand about Erik and what happened to him."

"There were a lot of things people didn't talk about in those days, Sarah. The fact that your grandmother kept these journals is remarkable. Many people could barely read or write, so their stories have been lost forever."

"How could they not know about Erik when he lived in the house with them?" I wondered.

"What your grandmother experienced was not unusual, Sarah. The young girls that worked in the big houses were very vulnerable. Most of them were little more than children when they were sent out to work. The women were in charge of the servants, and when things like that happened it was up to them to cover it up. Sadly, it was the master of the house who sometimes violated them, so secrecy was important to keep their standing in the community."

Frau Koenig was better than most," she continued. "She felt responsible for your grandmother, and was relieved, I think, that it had not been one of their friends who fathered Erik, or God forbid her husband. There was definitely the 'upper-class' in those days and she probably thought your grandmother was very naïve to think that Rauf loved her and would take responsibility for the child. That simply wasn't done. The fate of those girls and their children was most often what happened to that other girl. But it was wartime and with Herr Meyer's oldest son off fighting and Rauf gone, she may have harboured hopes that if Rauf knew about the child he would return."

"This is all so confusing."

"Yes, it is very strange." Lorna frowned and I suddenly felt guilty. I had not taken into consideration how learning about my family history may be bringing up unsettling memories of her own childhood and family background.

"What was your childhood like?" I asked.

She settled herself on the sofa and sighed as she sipped her tea.

"Seligenstadt was very much like your grandmother's home. All the major cities in Germany had farmland surrounding them, and settlements where people lived who helped service the farms. My father fought in the war and returned a different man. I was born in 1922 when things were better after the war ended, but many people were malnourished and weak. It wasn't until years later that I found out I had a brother born in 1920 who only lived a few days. My mother wasn't strong, and he had little chance of survival.

My father never talked about the war or much of anything else. The men were expected to go back to their lives as if nothing happened, I guess. It was a difficult life for them and a daily grind just to provide food. The men who fought were heroes certainly, but not the only ones. Those who worked the farms to keep the troops fed were heroes in their own right. Especially as it cost them dearly in not having enough food for their own families. Many of them never really regained their strength and were burdened with the disability of having lived such a life.

Things did improve over the years, but times were still hard and in 1938 there was talk of war again. My parents were horrified at the thought. Some family friends had a daughter my age named Giselle and they decided to send her to England, so they arranged for me to go with her. I was sixteen. I begged and pleaded with them not to send me away, especially as England was no friend to Germany in those days. But they had made up their minds."

"What happened in England?" I asked gently.

"Giselle was being sent to live with an aunt in London. This aunt had married an Englishman some years before. I'm not sure if I ever knew how she came to marry this man, but she had lived in London for a long time. She was not expecting two young girls to show up, but she took us both in. For the first year or so we worked in a hospital doing manual tasks like cleaning up and helping wherever we could. It was unpleasant and tedious work, but we learned the English language. She then arranged for us to work at Selfridges Department Store on Oxford Street, which was a welcome change from the hospital."

"Is that where you learned to be such a fashionable woman, Lorna?" I asked. "You have such good taste."

Lorna laughed. "We were country girls from a small village. Everyone knew each other and all the families helped each other by exchanging clothing as their children outgrew things. One winter I wore a coat that had been worn by three girls before me and was grateful to have it. We had no idea what was fashionable, we only cared if the garment fit and was warm for winter."

"The customers we waited on at Selfridges were obviously women of means and even though it was wartime, there were still social engagements and these women had to look their best. Some of them had a horrible taste."

She laughed again and I could see memories flash across her face. "Giselle had a knack for knowing what looked good on different types of women and the talent to direct them to styles that worked for them. I don't know where it came from, but the customers liked her, and she became very popular. I watched her closely and learned from her." Lorna sighed and reached forward to set her cup on the coffee table. I offered her more tea, but she declined.

"Giselle and I were more comfortable living in London by this time, and we ventured out to the dance halls and places where young people congregated. There were always soldiers around the city and it was an exciting time." She noticed my expression. "As strange as it sounds, the early days of the war had their own brand of excitement. It was like static in the air and soldiers came and went at a steady pace. I have to admit that we had fun during those early days of the war."

"Is that how you met Frank?"

"Frank was a Canadian soldier working Intelligence, so he did not see combat. We met at a dance early in 1940 and things were fine at first, but we barely escaped the Blitz later that year. He was called back to Canada shortly after the Blitz ended to report on the status of Great Britain and her allies. He didn't want to leave me, not knowing if or when he would return, so we married, and I came with him to Canada."

She seemed to look deep into herself. "He was stationed in London again in 1943, but I remained in Canada. Daniel was born while Frank was overseas, so they didn't actually meet until Daniel was six months old." She smiled weakly.

"Giselle stayed on in London and Frank tried to find her when he returned. The house where we lived with her aunt had been destroyed and it wasn't until sometime later that he learned she had died in 1944 in an air raid."

I looked at this poised, beautiful woman and realized that everyone has a story. My generation has no idea what these people lived through. I was beginning to understand why people who live through such adversity do not want to look back. My admiration for her had steadily grown over the weeks since we started this project and even though she was twice my age I had come to think of her as a friend.

"I'm so sorry, Lorna if helping me with this has made you remember sad times in your life."

"Don't be, Sarah. If my parents had not shipped me off to England, I would not have met Frank. We were married for over forty years and had two wonderful children. I got my teaching certificate here in Canada and enjoyed many years as a teacher. My parents were physically and mentally much older than their years, and as much as I would have liked to stay with them, I probably would not have survived the war if I had stayed. It was when I had children of my own that I fully realized the sacrifices they made for me."

She smiled. "The majority of my life has been full and happy, Sarah, and perhaps the adversities faced as a young woman helped me grow and mature."

I nodded. "You are helping me see my parents in a different light, too. They don't like to share the past either. My father didn't go to war as he has a slight heart murmur, easily controlled with medication now, but he was also needed in the factory as they made boots for the soldiers being deployed to Europe."

We sat in silence for a few moments until Zipper wandered into the living room and jumped up on the sofa, breaking the mood.

I got the box and removed the final journal. It was thicker than the other two. I also took out the packet of letters and showed them to Lorna. We undid the ribbon and opened one of them. The paper was very thin, and the writing was difficult to read.

"I don't expect you to translate these letters, Lorna. Hopefully, the last journal will explain the rest of the story." I took out the velvet bag and showed her the wedding ring, explaining that this had not been the one my grandmother had worn.

Lorna took the last journal, the letters, and the remaining cassettes. She said she would call me when she returned from Arizona.

"I won't take any of this with me," she said, "so it may be a while before I finish it."

"Safe travels, Lorna, and thank you for everything." I bent to pick up Zipper to hide the tears in my eyes. Her eyes glistened too as she tickled Zipper under his chin and waved goodbye.

Chapter Eleven

MY MOM

EARLY IN MARCH, the gang got together at *Frogs*. Katie and Ian joined us again and my neighbours, Doug and Laura came out as well. John and Dana had gone to the Bahamas for Valentine's Day and came home engaged. We were *oohing* and *awing* over her engagement ring when Ro arrived with Ben. She apologized for not being there early as her sitter had been late. It did not go unnoticed that she was seeing Ben on a weekend when Joey was home with her.

All attention turned to Ben, whom we were meeting for the first time. He seemed a bit nervous as introductions were made. In response to the questions peppered at him, he told us that he had been in South America for a few years working on a big project but was home now involved in something new and starting a business. He looked relieved when the attention went back to John and Dana.

Katie and I rose to go to the lady's room.

"Why do they always go in pairs?" Dean asked the table at large.

Katie and I smiled at each other in the mirror as we washed our hands.

"I really like your mom," I said reaching for paper towels.

"Yup, she's a keeper. She likes you too Sarah." She looked thoughtful for a moment. "It's funny but we seem to be closer since my dad passed away. I was close to both my parents, but they had their own life and friends. I see more of her now because she volunteers at the school these days. It must be a big adjustment to be single again after all those years." She smiled again. "She's enjoying translating those letters for you. How is that going?"

"Good," I said putting my lipstick back in my purse but saying no more about it. I had not spoken of the box with anyone except Ro.

"Mom should be back from Arizona next week," Katie said, combing her hair.

"My parents aren't due back until the end of the month. Lorna reminds me of my mom. They seem to have the same taste and both wear scarves with everything."

She laughed. "She must have a million scarves. Do you think we will ever be able to pull off that look?"

We were both laughing as we returned to the table to find the guys all down at one end talking about South America with Ben. The girls were clustered at the other end discussing wedding plans with Dana. We joined the discussion about white or cream for a wedding dress.

"After all we have been living together," said Dana.

Later I was thinking about what Katie said. My mother and I had a good relationship too and I missed both her and my father. We talked on the phone often, but I was looking forward to them being home, especially as I wanted to discuss the things I was discovering about my grandmother's past.

Lorna called the following week. She was home busy catching up but would get back to the journal in a few days. I told her I needed a new spring coat and asked her to go shopping with me. "Sure" she agreed, and I said I would pick her up on Saturday morning. She pulled a yellow quilted raincoat from the rack. "This would look great with your hair Sarah."

"Yellow?" I wondered taking the coat from her and studying it.

She stood behind me as I tried it on as we both looked in the mirror. "You look like sunshine on a cloudy day," she said. "Isn't that from the song My Girl?" We both laughed as I turned around to check the back. "Hey, look it has a hat," I said reaching into the pocket. "Well, that's it then." Taking off the coat I slung it over my arm and picked up the hanger.

We moved on to sweaters and Lorna chose one in a coral shade. "This will go perfectly with a scarf I bought in Arizona," she said. I laughed remembering my conversation with Katie. "It will also match that gorgeous tan you're wearing," I said as we headed to the checkout.

We were both humming 'My Girl' as we waited in line to pay for our items.

We didn't mention the journal until I dropped Lorna off a few hours later. She said she would call me when she had finished the translation.

I talked to my parents regularly over the winter, but most of our conversations were of the 'checking in' nature. They called on a Sunday afternoon in mid-March to tell me that they planned to make their return trip more of an adventure than just a trek north on the interstate. My dad chatted for a few minutes and then handed the phone over to my mom.

"Your dad is driving me crazy, Sarah. He's got the map out and has spent days, literally days, mapping out our return trip. I keep telling him that we need to get home, but he insists that we should see a few of the states on the way. We haven't even set up the condo in Etobicoke yet."

I could hear her frustration but knowing my dad I didn't think she had much of a chance of changing his mind.

On the twenty-second of March, the receptionist buzzed me to say my father was on the line.

"Dad?" I asked, surprised that he would call me at work.

"Sarah, I have some terrible news," he started, sounding out of breath. "Your mother fell on the golf course and—and—she passed away this afternoon!"

"What?" I said standing up behind my desk. There was a pause, and another voice came on the line.

"Sarah, it's Frank Henderson, your dad has gone to sit down."

"What's happening?" I manage to whisper.

"We were on the golf course and your mother collapsed. The people behind us raced off to the clubhouse on their cart but by the time help arrived it was too late."

"We're still at the hospital and the doctor says he thinks it was an aneurysm. They've given your dad something to relax him. Brenda and I are taking him home with us. Here write down our number and we will talk later, okay?"

I scribbled his phone number on a piece of paper and gently hung up the phone. Shaking, I went to the lady's room and ran cold water over my hands. I felt like I was in a daze but went around to reception.

"Donna, did my dad just call here?" I asked.

"Yes, he did just a few minutes ago. Did you lose the call? Do you want me to try to get him back?" she asked reaching for the phone.

"No, it's all right," I said turning to go back to my office.

"Sarah, are you all right? Is there anything I can do for you?"

"No, no I don't think so," I mumbled as I made my way back to my office.

I dialled my boss and explained what happened. He offered any help I might need. I knew Linda was in a meeting, so I scribbled a hasty note, put it on her desk, and left the office.

Dave was easy to reach at the clinic in Mississauga, but there was no answer at the loft in Montreal. I had no idea how to reach Mike, so I called Marc at the restaurant. Marc offered condolences and said he knew where Mike was working and would get in touch with him right away. No more than fifteen minutes later Mike called back and said he would call me later when he got home.

I called Frank Henderson back and he said they had taken Dad home with them. He was badly shaken but the sedative he had been given at the hospital had worked and he was lying down. I told Frank I had talked to both my brothers, and we were trying to determine what to do. I said I would call him back later. Over the next few hours and several phone calls back and forth, it was agreed that I would go to Florida. I booked a flight for the following day and wondered what to do next.

Getting my thoughts together I went to the bedroom to pack a bag when Ro called and said she had been trying to get through to me. Linda had called and told her the news, but said she had not been able to reach me either. I told her what happened, and she offered to come with me, but I insisted she shouldn't as it would likely upset Joey. I was preparing a cup of tea when Laura knocked on my side door.

"Sarah, I'm so sorry. Ro just called me. Can I do anything for you?"

We sat at the dining room table and talked for a bit. Zipper was purring on my lap when Mike called again. Laura motioned 'call me' as she went out the side door. Mike had spoken to Dad and was worried about his state of mind. He said Dave had called Dad too and was also worried.

My boss told me to take all the time I needed, and Laura said she would look after Zipper while I was gone.

Frank picked me up at the airport and drove me to the house where Brenda was waiting with Dad. He had spent the night with them but was now back in his home. Over the next number of hours, several people dropped in with food and offered condolences. Dad was clearly in shock, so I took over greeting people and taking phone calls. No one ate much, but food just kept coming.

It was three days before everything was sorted out. The funeral director was very gracious, but the paperwork seemed endless. We had no idea how complicated it is when someone dies outside of the country. It certainly wasn't anything we had discussed when my parents decided to buy a home in Florida. It was decided that Mom would be cremated and her remains would be sent to a funeral home in Etobicoke near the condo. Dad broke down in the funeral director's office when he told us her urn would have to go through customs to enter Canada.

I wondered how often this happened and guessed a lot with the number of Snowbirds in Florida every winter. The funeral director and his staff were well versed in what to do and had all the necessary forms. The arrangements were made seamlessly while Dad and I sat helplessly waiting for the nightmare to be over. When we got back to the house, Dad's pallor was grey and he again went to lie down. I talked to the boys and told them I was going to bring Dad back with me the next day.

I put the kettle on for a cup of tea and went to the fridge for milk when I noticed all the food in the fridge.

Having Dad fly back with me was the right thing to do. I couldn't leave him in Florida in the state he was in, but it occurred to me that the house would have to be closed for the season. His car was sitting in the driveway and what would we do with all this food? Frank and Brenda arrived to find me staring into the fridge. Brenda made tea and we sat in the sunroom. I told them everything about the arrangements and that I wanted to fly Dad home with me the next day. They agreed it was the best thing to do.

"I don't know what we will do about the house and Dad's car," I said. "We hadn't even thought about all that, with everything that has been going on. And all that food in the fridge." I shook my head. There was just so much to consider.

"We don't want you to worry about that, Sarah," said Frank. "We will look after the house and drive your dad's car back. We'll be leaving in a few weeks. We just ask that you wait until we return to have the memorial service for your mother."

I had shed some tears over the previous days, but at that point, I just broke down completely. Brenda consoled me while Frank went to find brandy.

"I can't ask you to take care of everything here and drive the car back," I said when I recovered and slowly sipped a glass of brandy.

"You didn't ask, we offered," said Brenda. "But it would be such an inconvenience for you to have to drive his car back."

I protested, but they said they would take an extra day or so if need be and we shouldn't worry about it.

They had to close their own home for the season and insisted it was no big deal to do the same for Dad.

I booked flights for Dad and me for the next day and insisted that Frank take a cheque from me to cover the cost of gas, motels, and meals for the trip back. I suggested that Dad stay with me for a few days, but I think he was just exhausted and wanted to be in his own environment. Ro had asked me for his condo keys and she and Dana had stocked his fridge and freshened things up a bit. Not for the first time in my life I marvelled at how fortunate we were to have such genuine friends.

Laura saw me pull into the driveway and came over a bit later with Zipper.

I drove Dad around for a few days and offered him my car, but he said he was fine. I had been away from the office for almost a week and had to check in. The boys called Dad every day and I tried to make sure he had meals. Ro, Dana, and Linda had all dropped off food for him, but he wasn't eating much.

We held a service for Mom late in April. Mike flew in from Montreal. We shared memories with friends, former colleagues, in-laws, and other family members. My brother's friends came, and my friend group rallied around me. Lorna came with Katie and Ian, and I introduced them to my family. The day was a haze of hugs, soft sentiments, and gentle touches but I doubt if I will remember any of it.

Gradually life returned to a sense of normal. I still called Dad every night and the boys checked in regularly, but life had to go on. Lorna called a few times, but we did not discuss the box until almost the end of May. I did want to close the lid on that, so to speak, and we agreed to meet at my house again. This time it was just Lorna and me, as Ro was not available.

Chapter Twelve

MANHATTAN

On May 31, 1917, Rauf and I are married in Jersey City, New Jersey in the United States of America. We are happy, but the way here has been difficult.

I got caught sending my letter to Rauf. I lived in the Koenig household for five years and have never stolen anything, but I took a few coins from a pouch in the kitchen meant for Cook to pay for deliveries and things she needs, to pay for the postage. Cook sees and knows everything, but I had to take the chance.

There are discussions about America joining Great Britain as an ally and anything to do with America was of interest to the men in the Koenig house. The Postmaster was questioned, and his clerk was punished, but my letter had gone to Rauf before it happened.

Herr Koenig and Herr Meyer question me for hours. Cook found my letter from Rauf, and it sits on the dining room table. I know they have read it. The truth comes out about Erik. Herr Meyer demands that I bring Erik to him. I find him hidden behind a cupboard in the kitchen and Cook glares at me as I pick him up in my arms.

He has had his second birthday but is a quiet and timid boy, thin and pale. His eyes are huge with fright as I take him to the dining room.

Herr Meyer's face is red with rage as he screams at me.

"This, this is Rauf's son?" He points his finger at Erik. Erik is terrified and turns his face into my shoulder. He is shaking and puts his thumb in his mouth.

Herr Koenig says nothing but looks confused and angry. I think he does not even know that Erik exists and has been living in his house all this time. Frau Koenig appears in the dining room and sees the letter on the table.

Her husband yells at her. "Did you know about this?"

I think he feels foolish in front of Herr Meyer. Frau Koenig wrings her hands and says, "Yes, Ava told me that Rauf is Erik's father, but I did not know that he has written to her."

He is furious with Frau Koenig, and I step back, holding Erik tighter. I am afraid that her kindness and her failure to disclose everything to her husband will cause her a great deal of grief.

Erik is hiccupping frantically into my shoulder in an effort not to cry and his little body is shaking violently. Frau Koenig calls Cook who is listening at the door to come to take Erik away. I think she is afraid for him.

Herr Koenig is trying to calm his friend down, but Herr Meyer is in a rage. He turns his rage to Herr Koenig and says, "I will not return to this house with that girl here," pointing at me. "How do we know this child is Rauf's? She could be making this all up."

"Rauf is in America," Frau Koenig says pointing at the letter. Herr Meyer grasps his chest, and his face gets redder and redder.

"You knew he is in America?"

Frau Koenig says nothing and her husband glares at her. This is his household and yet, he knew none of this.

Herr Koenig turns to me and shrieks, "Get out, get out of my house." Frau Koenig covers her face with her hands, and I know she can do nothing to help me.

I rush through the kitchen and find Cook in my room throwing our meagre belongings into a sack. Erik is under the bed and when I pick him up, he feels lifeless. His face is as pale as snow and his eyes are closed, and he is breathing in a hollow way.

Cook grabs my arm and says, "Quick, go hide in the garden shed. I will come to you when my work is done." She grabs my shawl and the blanket from my bed to wrap around Erik.

I have no idea why Cook tells me to do this, but I am in such a state of distress I do as she says. It is freezing cold in the shed, but I wrap Erik and myself in the blanket and wait. Finally, Cook appears.

"Come with me but be very quiet."

She takes to me to her house, which is near the harbour. Her daughter Antje is there with a small child perhaps a year older than Erik. They make tea and broth which helps to warm us a bit, but Erik is still in shock.

Cook tells me that Antje's husband has been killed in the war. They have friends who had left for New York and

Cook wants her to go there for safety. Cook knows people who work at the harbour, and she says there is a ship coming from America in a few weeks. She has arranged for Antje to go to New York on this ship as a maid, but they will not take her child.

"I cannot look after her child. I must work all day. This must be done in secrecy, so we cannot ask anyone else. But you could go in her place."

My mind is in turmoil, and I cannot think.

"But if they will not take her child, how could I take Erik?"

"You would leave Erik here. There is payment for duties as a maid on this ship. When you get to New York you will send us the money and Antje could bring both children. She could travel as a widow with two small children if she has the fare. It is risky and if America does enter the war as an ally to Great Britain the ports will be closed. We will not have another chance."

I stare at her in disbelief. "You want to join Rauf in America, so here is your chance. What else can you do?"

"I will find another placement as a maid."

"Ha! Do you think Herr Meyer will let that happen?"

"Then I will take Erik and return to Wernigerode."

"The villages are suffering now. Food from the farms is being sent to the city and the army. People are trying to get by, but they are starving. Do you really think they can take you and Erik in and have the loss of your wages too?"

I think of my sister with her household already full of people and the shame this would bring upon my family. They will indeed be in worse conditions without my wages, and Erik and I will just add to the problems. I cannot give

Cook an answer, but she says we can stay with her for a few days.

How could I leave Erik? Even if I take him to another city and find work, which may not be possible, who will take care of him? We spend the next few days alone with Antje and her daughter while Cook is working. Antje is quiet and timid, especially around Cook. But she is calm and takes good care of her daughter. Erik slowly starts to feel better and does not cling to me so much. He has never been around other young children and seems to be interested in Antje's small daughter. She seems to understand Erik and does not pressure him.

I know that Cook will not let us stay much longer. We are a burden to her, and I am careful to take what little shelter and food she offers, but I know she wants me to make up my mind soon. I hold Erik in our cot at night and watch him as he sleeps, but I cannot sleep myself because of worry.

Cook comes home with talk of how upset things are in the Koenig household. Frau Koenig and the children are nowhere to be seen and Herr Koenig and Herr Meyer are raging at each other. I think that maybe Antje will care for Erik if I find another job, but anyone who would hire me would be friends of the Koenigs and Meyers. I know that Cook is right and that it won't happen.

I start to think that this may be the best thing for Erik as well as myself. My poor little boy is not growing as he should. He does not speak and is alone most of the time. His toys are stones from the garden, and he eats very little. I share my food with him, but it is not enough to keep both of us healthy. Antje takes good care of her daughter and I know she will care for Erik. He may be happy with another child to play with.

Rauf has not forgotten me and if my letter reaches him, he will know that he has a son. It could be months before I see Erik again, but when we are reunited, Rauf and I will give him all the love we have.

The voyage across the ocean is a nightmare for me. No one seems to care who I am, just that I do what is asked of me. But within a few days, I am so sick I can hardly stand. It is worse at night when I lay down, so I cannot rest. This ship is carrying cargo but also has passengers. My duties are to clean the dining room and the cabins. I am glad that I do not have to serve meals as I am so unsteady on my feet, I think I will spill food on everyone.

The passengers are wealthy people. I hear talk that there are 'certain people' who wanted to get out of Germany. I do not know what was meant by that, only that these people must have money to pay for their passage. I worry that my wages will not be enough to cover the fare for Antje and the children.

I share my sleeping room with a woman named Sophia who is a cook on the ship. Our room is small, with two cots and a bit of space to walk between. Sophia is getting upset with me because I am disturbing her sleep, too. She is about ten years older than me and Italian, but can speak some German so we can talk a bit. After a week of this, she tells me that she has seen men twice my size that cannot carry on their work being as seasick as I am.

She helps me by pressing her thumbs above my eyes and at the back of my neck, which strangely eases my stomach. She tells me to relax my body and go with the motion rather than fighting it. She also makes me some broth as I cannot eat solid food and will reach out in the night to put her hand on my shoulder to steady me. I feel a little better but every time I look out, all I see is black water, rolling waves, and a sky of clouds. It is very cold with freezing rain falling day and night.

We learn that the ship must venture south to avoid rough February seas and the trip will take longer than normal. This continues for days, and I start to think that America does not exist.

Sophia becomes friendlier and tells me that her family has all been living in America for several years, except for a few older relatives who stayed behind in Italy. She lives with her mama and brother in a place called Manhattan. I explain that I must get to New Jersey. She has cousins there and knows it well.

Finally, the day comes when land is in sight. Sophia points out the Statue of Liberty as we approach the harbour. I am weak but relieved. I can hardly walk on land; I am so used to the rolling of the ship. Someone approaches but Sophia tells him we are crew from the ship. He loses interest and does not even look at me as he thinks we are both Americans returning from the voyage. I have been on board that ship under Antje's name, so no one even knows who I am. Lucky they do not seem to care. Sophia takes me on a train travelling underground, filled with people. There are no seats so we must stand. I am sick again but soon we reach her home. They live in an apartment in a large building full of people. We must walk up four flights of stairs and many people are passing us going up and down. This building is full of strange smells, and I fear I will stumble and fall.

Finally, Sophia opens a door, and a large woman greets her. This is her mama, Maria. She looks at me and they start to speak rapidly in Italian. I do not understand what they are saying, only that Maria is questioning her about me. I feel so sick that I collapse on the floor.

When I wake, I do not know where I am. The room is small with two beds, and I think I am still on the ship. Strange smells are coming from the kitchen, and I gasp. Maria comes into the room drying her hands on her apron. She is smiling, but I shrink back in fear. She sits beside me on the bed and gently wipes my face and talks to me. I cannot understand what she is saying, but her voice is gentle and gradually I begin to relax. I am so weak I would not be able to do anything to help myself, but I feel she means me no harm. She brings me some tea and I sleep again.

Gradually I begin to feel better. Maria is the only one there during the day and she spends all her time in the kitchen. Sophia works in her uncle's restaurant when she is not on a ship, and I meet her brother Carlos who drives a delivery truck for a fish market. In the evening people are always coming into the apartment and everyone spends time in the kitchen. I begin to eat and find that the strange smells have become more appealing.

One day there is no one at home. I do not know where Maria has gone but I find a mop, some rags, and a pail in the cupboard and clean the apartment. I am still weak, but the work is satisfying, and I feel I am repaying them in a small way for their generosity. Maria hugs me when she returns and tells me I am a good girl.

Sophia gives me an envelope with some money. She tells me these are my wages from the ship. She took the envelope as she thought I would be robbed in the state that I was in. I give some of the money to Maria as I do not want to feel I am a burden to her.

I have been in Sophia's home for several weeks and my story comes out a little bit at a time. Sophia tells me that the money I earned on the ship is far less than the cost of passage for Antje and the children. She also tells me that there is much talk of America joining the conflict, and if that happens there will be no ships sailing to and from Germany. I cry for Erik and regret my foolishness forever thinking this plan would work.

Chapter Thirteen

NEW JERSEY

I tell Maria and Sophia that I must get to New Jersey to find Rauf. Carlos says he will go there in a week to make deliveries and he will take me. I tell him I must find 97 Dwight Street.

He takes me with him to New Jersey and I wait in the truck while he makes his deliveries. At one restaurant they give Carlos some food and he shares it with me. When his deliveries are done, he takes me to Dwight Street. We get out of the truck, and I see a long row of houses attached to each other. There is a long stairway to the door, which is repeated many times down the street. There are people everywhere, children playing in the street and women talking in groups with babies on their hips. I know that Rauf lives in apartment 2B. We go into the building and find that door, but no one answers when we knock.

Carlos tells me we will wait in his truck where it is warm. Many more people crowd the street as men are returning from their work. I look and look, but do not find Rauf. Carlos tells me he must return the truck to Manhattan but does not want to leave me there alone. He drives a few blocks away and points out the home of one of their cousins. He takes a scrap of the wrapping paper from our meal and makes a note.

"I will take you back to Dwight Street and you wait inside the building by Rauf's door. If he does not come, you will go to the cousins. Give them this note."

He hands it to me, and I put it deep inside my pocket. I am frightened, but I cannot ask more of Carlos. I sit by the door and watch as more people arrive. They stare at me, but no one talks to me. I am frantic but do not want to leave. It is dark in the street and still I wait. Finally, I see a man coming up the stairs and know it is Rauf.

"Ava!" He looks at me in surprise and shock as I stand to greet him. "I cannot believe you are really here!" He takes me in his arms, and I start to cry in relief.

The German man named William that shares his flat returns shortly after. He is surprised to see me there. Rauf has spoken to him about me, but he does not seem pleased to see me. Over the next few days, I explain everything about how I have come to America, how Sophia's family took me in as I was so sick, and about Erik.

We are married, but my reunion with Rauf is not as I expected at first. I realize that I barely know him. The spoiled rich boy with dreams and ambitions has been replaced by a man now living a very different life. He is working long hours, six days a week, and he is weary when he comes home.

William is resentful and sullen and barely speaks to me. He works long hours in a shoe factory, so he is away most of the time, too, but when he is home, he treats me as an intruder. The flat is not big enough for the three of us, and it is awkward. I spend my days alone filled with worry and I wonder many times if I have done the right thing. But I try to make a home for us.

One Sunday, a few weeks later there is a knock on the door, and we find Carlos standing there. He tells us he has Maria and Sophia with him, and they are going to the cousins, and we must come too. The cousin's house is filled with people and Maria and Sophia hug me tight. There is a lot of noise, everyone is talking and laughing. Rauf and I are quickly accepted by this wonderful family. The women are in the kitchen and the men are in the small garden chasing the children around and talking. These are beautiful people, with their dark shiny hair and bright dark eyes. We spend a happy day with them, but after the meal is over the talk turns serious. The women chase the men back outside while we clean up and tend to the children.

Rauf tells me that America is preparing to enter the war any day. We have talked about Erik many times, but we do not know how to bring him to America. The ports are closing and even if they were still open, we do not have enough money to pay for Antje's fare. We cannot contact her as the mail has stopped for many weeks now.

One of the cousins works in a hotel in New Jersey and she tells me I can get a job there as a maid. I am worried as I do not speak English but find there are women from all countries there. I know how to clean and that is all that matters. My days are full now and I am helping to save money to bring Erik to us. My relationship with Rauf improves now that I am busy.

William finds a room with an elderly couple on the third floor, but he continues to spend time with us. He is still sullen, but the situation is better.

In April 1917 America joined the Alliance Power and rushes to support them in Europe. Carlos and some of the cousins have been in America for many years and have become citizens so they must go to fight.

Rauf and William are not American citizens, so they are not required to go, but are busier than ever in the factories. The textile factory is making uniforms and the shoe factory is making boots for the army.

We still go to the cousins every Sunday, but the house is no longer filled with laughter. Many of the women are working in the factories and some of the shine in their hair and eyes is gone. Maria and Sophia have moved to the cousins, as they can no longer afford to stay in Manhattan with Carlos gone. Sophia is working in another restaurant, and Maria tends to the children while the women are in the factories all day.

Despite everything, Rauf and I are happy and have made a home for ourselves. By autumn I am pregnant again. This time it is different as I am among people who care for me and I for them. Sophia has become the friend I never had, and Maria is everyone's mother, including mine. Food is not plentiful, but I am learning to cook the Italian way, and pasta is sustaining all of us. Rauf and I are saving as much as we can for the day the war is over, but we also help Sophia and Maria.

Rauf feels guilty as he has escaped the war twice, by fleeing Germany before it began and now in America. But he is also horrified at the thought of fighting his own countrymen in Germany, so he is glad he has not been called to go.

On May 24, 1918, we welcome another son that we name Rauf to honour his papa. I stay home with him for a few months and watch him grow. The cousins give us clothes and toys from their children and when I return to the hotel, he has many children around him, and Maria to love him. I think every day of Erik in Germany and hope that he is as fortunate.

November 11, the war to end all wars is over! The streets are filled with people, yelling, and singing, celebrating with victory. We are sad for our motherland, but again, hope that we can finally be united with Erik. He will soon be four years old. We write to Antje and Greta for news of Erik and my family in Wernigerode.

Everyone is looking to the harbour for signs of their sons, brothers, and husbands' return, but it takes months before ships start to appear. The ships are filled with men returning to America. Some are taken right to the trains for transport to their homes in other parts of the country. Families crowd the harbour when news of a ship is received. Some of them are joyful but many return to their homes with empty hearts. There is no way to know if their men will return on another ship, or not at all.

Chapter Fourteen

SPANISH FLU

A FEW OF the cousins return. These strong, handsome Italian men have been replaced with mere shadows of their former selves. All the men getting off the ships look like that, and we are shocked. We are starting to understand that the war is over, but another enemy is taking its place. These men are sick and all the love and care we are giving them is not making them well again. One cousin who was full of life and fun sits in the garden growing weaker every day while his wife cries in the kitchen. The children are afraid of him.

Then other people start to get sick, and we hear of something called the Spanish flu. Families moved in together when the men were gone, and houses now have many people living in small spaces. The hotels are full of men being housed there until they can be transported to other states. We cannot keep the hotel clean, as the men come and go quickly. The train station is bursting with men returning to their homes in other states, but some must wait until there is room. They sleep in the station, on the benches, and on the floor, with no place to wash or find food. When a train arrives, they are fighting to get on, to go home, but the trains are overcrowded.

The flu is spreading quickly, and people start to die in big numbers. The government declared quarantine when the ships arrived, and we must all wear masks. Many businesses have closed, but the factories remain open, and the hotels are busier than ever.

One day a neighbour of the cousins came to tell them of Carlos. He fought with Carlos and had seen him die on the battlefield. No one knew where he is buried. When I learned of this, I run to Maria. I hold her in my arms to comfort her the way she comforted me when I first came to America. But then her body had been warm and soft and felt like a pillow as she rocked me. Now she felt thin and frail, and her hair is almost white.

I tell her that Carlos was a hero on both sides of the ocean; how he shared his food with me and made sure I was safe the day he brought me to New Jersey. But she cannot be consoled. I think of all the mothers who would never know their son's final resting place. I cried with her for all the lost sons, including my own. I have no way to know if Erik is alive and safe.

The city is in lockdown. The streets that were filled with people are now quiet and strange. We may go only to work, and the police are watching that everyone is wearing a mask. We can no longer take our son to Maria, instead, a woman in our building takes care of him while we are gone. We do not go to the cousins on Sundays anymore, so Rauf and I spend our time at home. We grow closer and enjoy our young son. He has his first birthday and is happy and growing strong.

Then we learn that Maria has become sick. We wait for more news but when it arrives, we are heartbroken to learn she has died. I sneak to the cousins and find that Sophia is broken. She must now take Maria's place as mama to everyone, but she is stricken and looks much older than her years.

Months pass and it gets worse and worse. Many people are dying, and no one can stop it. Rauf and I cling to each other and hope and pray. We begin to think that maybe we can go to Germany and bring Erik back with us, but no one can travel at this time. We save more and more, with the hope that the day will come when we can make this happen.

To our horror Rauf becomes sick. We do not leave our flat. I do not go to the hotel. I nurse him day and night, but he does not get better. He dies early one Sunday morning just as the sun is starting to rise.

I do not know what to do. Who will look after young Rauf if I get sick and die? I cannot bear the thought of him being left behind, as Erik has been. The children did not seem to be as affected by the sickness, but what would I do if I lost another son? I am heartbroken and more frightened than ever.

William remained aloof, but one day he comes to me and says we need to get out of New Jersey. He says there are too many people here who are sick and there is no escape from it. I ask him if he will go back to Germany, but he says no. The sickness is worse in Europe and Germany is in shambles since the war.

He wants to go to Canada, where he says things are much safer. He has heard of a shoe manufacturing factory that he can buy. It would be an opportunity for him. He tells me he will take me and my son with him, but that we must be married first. I am surprised by his proposal as he has never shown any affection to me or me toward him. I do not want to marry him, but he is persistent, and I start to think it is the only way.

Sofia breaks curfew and comes to see me. She learned that Rauf has died. She wears a mask and will not let me hug her. She tells me the sickness has reached their home and is afraid that she will give it to me. I do not think I have any more tears left, but Sophia and I cry together for everyone who is gone. I look at my dear, dear friend and see nothing but sadness in her. She says Maria, Carlos, and the others have earned their rest and are happy. She tells me she will join them soon as she is sick, too. But she is scared for the ones she will leave behind. She says if I stay, I will surely die.

I tell her of William's plan to go to Canada and his proposal to take me with him as his wife. I do not want to do this, but she tells me to look after myself and my young son. She says many women are left with children and no husbands. These women do not know what to do or how they will survive. She thinks that Canada has not been hit so hard by the sickness as the people are not living so close together.

I know that I must marry William to travel to Canada with him, but when he becomes my husband, he will take possession of the money Rauf and I worked so hard to save for Erik. He will use this money to buy the shoe factory and a home there. He promises me when we are settled, we will continue to try to bring Erik from Germany.

I am now living in Canada with a man I do not love. I was happy as Ava Baehr in Wernigerode and Hamburg before everything changed. Happier still as Ava Meyer in New Jersey with the man I loved, our young son, and hopes of reuniting with our firstborn. But now I am Ava Langner and living a different life.

I have no news of Germany and do not know if my family survived the war and the sickness. William's promise to help my family and bring Erik to us has disappeared. He will speak no more of it.

I lost another family, my Italian family. The last I hear of Sophia is that she has joined her mama, Carlos, and the others.

So, I am alone, but I have Rauf to look after, and I love him dearly. We are alive. William has little interest in me and less in the boy, but he did take us away from a place where we all may have perished.

I will not give up—I will find a way to discover what has happened to my family and help them if I can.

Chapter Fifteen

MAKING THE DECISION RIGHT

LORNA FOUND A picture in the pages of the last journal. She took it out and showed it to me. It was a black and white picture of a young man holding a small baby. I burst into tears as I look at the image. The man in it was obviously my paternal grandfather, tall, handsome, and smiling at the baby in his arms. I looked at Lorna and she was crying too. We sat at my dining room table for a bit and let the tears come. I was crying for the recent loss of my mother, the loss to my grandmother of this man she had loved and risked everything for, the life she had to endure, and the grandfather I had not known existed. Lorna is crying for me, but also for the loss of her parents, never knowing what had become of them. And for Frank, whom she still missed every day.

Mopping my face, I got a bottle of wine and two glasses, and invited Lorna into the living room. We sat there for several hours quietly talking as the afternoon sun changed the light in the room. Zipper curled up beside her on the sofa and she petted him gently as he snoozed.

"You would never have guessed what my grandmother went through if you had known her, Lorna. She was so good to us. We would have tea parties and she would bring out her best China cups. I can taste the almond cookies she baked. I have a few of her teacups, but I never use them, for fear of breaking them. Yet, she allowed me to use them as a young girl."

"Your grandmother was strong and brave and happy to have your family in her life. Perhaps she never wanted to look back, as it may have brought sadness and regret into her life." Lorna sighed. "I was mad at my parents for a long time. I never thought they didn't want me with them, but I was frightened and alone.

After I married Frank and came to Canada, I left my old life behind. I was young and took a chance with him, not knowing what kind of a future we would have. We had our ups and downs like every married couple, but we worked together and had a good life. If I had stayed with my parents, I likely would not have survived."

I nodded. "If my grandmother had not taken that leap of faith to come to America, her life may have ended as well. How hard it must have been to leave Erik there, with such an unknown future."

"*If*, one of the smallest words in the English language and yet one of the most powerful. Our fates would have been very different if they had taken other paths."

"*I wish*, is another one," I replied. "I wish I had known my real grandfather."

I told her about my brother, Mike, how artistic he is, and about his lifestyle. He had not 'come out' to my parents or Dave.

"Now that my mother is gone, he will never have that chance with her. I never really explained what happened in my marriage to her either."

"As parents, we are sometimes afraid to show frailties to our children, just as children don't want to expose things about their lives, thinking they will disappoint their parents. I don't think I ever told Katie or her brother Daniel about my parents or that I had an older brother who died."

I laughed. "What a delicate dance we perform for the people in our lives. And how strange those events we may not have even known about, play such a huge role in our lives."

"Frank and I wanted to go to Vancouver and spend time with Daniel and we also planned a trip to Europe. I wanted to go to Seligenstadt to see if I could find out what happened to my parents. We thought if we went there, we may have been able to find something."

"You still can do both those things, Lorna."

"Yes, I guess I can."

Before she left, she went to the dining room and looked at the letters in the box.

"Maybe the answer to Erik is in these letters, Sarah. Who knows, you may have family in Germany."

"I think it may be difficult to read them."

"Yes, you may be right, but I would like to try if you'll let me."

I gave her the letters, the tape recorder, and the rest of the cassettes.

"Lorna—"

"I know, Sarah." And she hugged me tightly.

Dad remained listless even though he had a lot of support around him. He went to Mississauga a few times to visit Dave and his family, and both my brothers called him regularly. His friends invited him to join them for various things, but he said he felt like a fish out of water without my mother. He and I fell into the habit of having dinner once a week. We would go out to eat, or sometimes I would cook, but it was difficult to draw him into a conversation. Mike told me he had invited Dad to Montreal for a visit, but he had yet to accept the invitation.

One Friday night I invited him to dinner but decided to take him to Frogs instead of eating at home. He was reluctant at first, but I told him I was hungry and had nothing prepared, so he had no choice.

Everyone was there, including Lorna. Katie and Ro were celebrating the end of the school year. The mood was fun, and Dad perked up a bit. The guys challenged him to a game of darts and shouts and laughter were coming from the game.

We always ate from everyone's plates and Dad laughed as a fight ensued over the last jumbo shrimp. He asked me who Lorna was and I explained her relationship to Katie but did not remind him that he had met her at Mom's funeral. I noticed them having a chat at one point in the evening.

He told me on the way home that he had enjoyed himself. He said he knew his friends were there for him, but he got the feeling he reminded them that they were all getting older and the same thing that happened to Mom could be waiting for them around the next corner.

Lorna mentioned to me that she had finished what she could with the letters, and they did provide insight into my grandmother's family and Erik. She said the letters were hard to read as they were written on very flimsy paper and the writing had faded over time. Greta was not as good at writing as my grandmother had been and wrote in disjointed sentences, so Lorna had just summarized the content of the letters rather than give me a one-to-one translation.

Chapter Sixteens

THE LETTERS

April 1924

Ava

Here is not so good. Papa suffered from the news of our brothers and had a fit. His arm and leg did not work, and his face became odd. They came to us and for weeks Papa sat in a chair by the window waiting for his sons to come home. One morning Mama finds him there and it is the end. Mama is not good. My husband got the sickness. He survives but has a heart problem and is too weak to work. Food is scarce, and I must do all the work in the garden to keep us eating, but it is spring, and will be a long time before our garden feeds us. We do not go to Hamburg so have no news of Erik.

We are eight people in my house, and I must look after everyone.

Greta

October 1924

Ava

We receive package from you with warm socks and hats. I find money and medicine hidden in socks. Medicine helps my husband. You tell me your new husband does not want Erik and does not want you to help us, but you do it.

Greta

February 1925

Ava

We receive coffee from you. We have not had coffee for long time. Find money and medicine hidden in the coffee. Also, children's shoes. Cook brings Erik to us. Antje's husband does not return from the war, but she finds another one. His wife dies from the sickness leaving him with young children. He takes Antje's daughter but will not take Erik, so she brings him to us. We have problems with him. My daughter's husband finds work driving a truck, so Erik has gone to work on Heinrich's farm. He does not speak and is small, but he helps on the farm, so Heinrich will keep him.

Greta

May 1926

Ava

The money you sent helps to buy some chickens. Our garden does better this year. Erik stays on Heinrich's farm. He does not make problems there. He works and sleeps in the barn and they feed him. My daughter's husband helps us. My husband works in the garden and feels better. Grandchildren are getting bigger and still need things.

Greta

April 1927

Ava

Mama died this year. She was an old lady and weak. My daughter and her husband are in their own home now. They still need things, so your packages help. Our garden does well, so we can eat more. We have not seen Erik this year, but Heinrich does not complain.

Greta

February 1929

Ava

You tell me you are coming to Hamburg so your husband can buy machinery for his factory. You will bring your son Rauf to meet us. You must not tell anyone about Erik. If your husband knows you help us, he will stop you. Erik is good on the farm, but still a strange boy. We do not want Heinrich to suffer because of you.

Greta

March 1931

Ava

My husband dies some months ago. I live with my daughter now and she takes care of me. I am weak and worn out, but I work in the garden, so that is good. More of the neighbourhood children are married and someone else lives in our home. I am happy to sit and knit with the wool that you send. You ask about Erik, but we do not see him. I think sometimes Heinrich forgets he is there; other than the help he gives him on the farm.

Greta

May 1936

Ava

We have learned that Erik dies. There was an accident on the farm, and he does not survive.

Greta

Chapter Seventeen

THE CALL OF THE LOONS

RO, JOEY, AND I spent a week at a cottage in Haliburton. The days were full of activity, and we all loved it. There was a canoe tied up at the dock and we found paddles, life jackets, and a grill for the firepit in a shed. After a good scrubbing Ro declared that the grill was suitable for cooking on our nightly bonfire. She relaxed Joey's diet that week and we grilled hamburgers and hot dogs on the fire, and s'mores and toasted marshmallows became a nightly ritual.

We shopped in the Village of Haliburton and returned to the cottage with flip-flops, hats, and a small fishing pole for Joey. He would fish from the end of the dock or troll, as Ro and I paddled around the bay in the canoe. One afternoon we paddled into a small inlet and heard loud splashing noises. We came upon beavers building a dam and splashing the water with their flat oval-shaped tails. Another day we took a hike along a trail behind the cottage and a snake crossed our path. Ro and I stepped back, but Joey was fascinated by it. I think it was nothing more than a common garter snake, but Joey was convinced it was a rattlesnake or a baby boa constrictor. Ro suggested Joey write a story about it and that evening he concocted a story about Simon the Snake and Bucky the Beaver complete with pictures.

The cottage had bunk beds in one bedroom. Joey called dibs on the top bunk and Ro slept in the bottom one. My bedroom had a lovely quilt folded on the end of the bed. I spread it out to admire the stitching and immediately thought of my grandmother who was never far from my thoughts those days.

We jumped off the dock and swam in the lake for hours. Joey got out of the water and said he wanted to go to the cottage for a minute to use the bathroom. Ro and I remained, chatting in the lake, but then realized he hadn't returned for some time. We hurried to the cottage; Ro went inside while I checked the shed to see if he was looking for something. She rushed out and yelled to me that she couldn't find him anywhere in the cottage. I told her to look again while I started down the trail, thinking he may have gone looking for the snake. I didn't get too far when I heard her call from my bedroom window. As I rushed to the window, she put her finger to her mouth and whispered a *shh* as I hurried inside. She had found him on his top bunk curled up fast asleep. He had pulled his sleeping bag over himself and was facing the wall, so she hadn't realized he was under it. He slept for two hours. We were sitting on the deck when he appeared yawning, his mop of curly hair in tangles. Ro pulled him close and kissed his forehead. I knew she was checking to see if he had a fever. He was fine and grumbled about her embrace.

"Joey, come over here," I invited. "I want a hug, too."

He grumbled some more but came to stand by my chair.

"Did you have a good nap?"

"I'm not a baby, I don't need naps" he complained.

"Even Superman needs downtime," I said.

He smiled at that and gave me a sleepy hug. Within a few minutes, he was back to his energetic self.

It rained one day, an all-day summer rain coming straight down, making circles on the lake with each drop. We found a Monopoly game on the bookshelf in the cottage and spent the whole day competing. Ro seemed to always pick the *Go to Jail, Do Not Pass Go, Do Not Collect $200* cards, and Joey and I would shriek with laughter each time it happened. We had the radio on, and the Haliburton station played the latest hits. Joey loved the *Bee Gees*, and he would imitate Barry Gibbs's falsetto voice whenever their songs were played. He was pretty good at it but when Ro and I joined in I don't think the Brothers Gibb would have been too impressed with our effort. Joey especially loved the song, *Tragedy*, and every time Ro ended up in jail, he and I would shout *Tragedy!*

We bought charcoal briquettes for the fire pit and after our meals, the coals would be perfect for roasting marshmallows. Joey would roast a few, but most evenings he would be nodding off by the time it got dark. Despite his Superman persona, he was just a little guy and needed his sleep. Ro would wash his sticky hands and face and tuck him in bed. Then she and I would retire to the deck with a glass of wine or on cooler nights a pot of tea, watch the fireflies, and listen to the night sounds of crickets and the occasional loon on the lake.

"They make such a forlorn or lost sound, don't they?" she remarked one night.

"Yes, it's like they are calling out to someone or something."

We sat in silence for a while, each lost in our thoughts. I brought the tape with the last journal and letters, that we had listened to the night before. I showed her the picture that had been tucked into the last journal.

"There's no doubt this man is your grandfather, your father looks just like him," Ro said as she filled our glasses with wine. "I've been thinking about how William tricked your grandmother into marrying him for her money."

I contemplated that for a few minutes.

"I know, Ro," I said, "and trust me, I never liked the man. But I've been thinking about that. Those were different times; women did not have the independence that you and I enjoy. I mean, we can get an education, own a home, and look after ourselves in ways my grandmother's generation could not. His motives were self-serving, but they did get her and my father out of a bad situation. I'm sure Sophia was right. There were many women like her, left with small children and husbands lost to the war or the Spanish flu."

"Yes, that's true," Ro admitted. "Do you think she would have gone back to Germany?"

"She might have, but I don't see how that would have been possible given the pandemic. I think marriage to William was her best option."

"I guess we'll never know." Ro paused for a moment.

"But the fact that he went back on his promise of using that money to help reunite her with Erik must have been quite a blow to her. He knew that she and Rauf were saving the money for that reason."

"That poor little boy," she said. "He never had a chance. It is the nature versus nurture argument, isn't it? I mean we don't know if there were problems when he was born or if he developed problems in early childhood. Can you imagine when they visited Germany and she couldn't claim him as her son?"

"You know the expression 'it takes a village to raise a child'? I have a Village." Ro touched my arm and continued. "Joey and I had a lot of support right from the beginning. And he was in daycare and had stimulation from other kids from a young age. I have summers off and could take him to things like Mommy and Me groups, swimming lessons, and day camps. Your grandmother had nothing like that with Erik."

She shook her head. "Her Italian family was her village in New Jersey when your father was a baby, but she lost that, too."

"She must have been a very strong woman." I sighed. "But I never knew her as being bitter or remorseful. I'm sure she had regrets, but she was such a loving and caring woman, and she found ways to help her family, despite Williams's objections. The fact that she had hidden this information away suggests that he never knew she was helping them. I don't think Greta would have mentioned it when they visited."

"Yes, she gets high marks for that. She probably squirrelled away money without William knowing. Greta appears to be quite bitter, at least in her early letters. I don't think your grandmother ever told her the whole story. Even though Rauf was a rich man's son, he certainly wasn't living that way in New Jersey. And it is obvious that Greta didn't know the circumstances that led her to marry William, or that it was her and Rauf's money that gave him his start in Canada. I wonder what happened to her. There were no more letters after 1936, were there?"

"Not that I know of, but it would be interesting to know what happened to her and the rest of the family. The second world war started just a few years later, so it is very possible they didn't make it through that time."

"Pearls on a string."

"What?"

"Oh, that's something Lorna said. The '*Ifs*' in life. Maybe call it fate. Each pearl is an event or person that lines up with the next one. If none of this had happened, I wouldn't be here with you and Joey."

Ro nodded. "You're a Pearl on Joey's string, Sar." She laughed. "Most single women our age would take a holiday somewhere interesting and exotic and yet here you are."

"I enjoy spending time with Joey, Ro."

"I know, but more importantly he knows, and will remember these times when he is older."

"Maybe someday we will all spend time in interesting and exotic places," I replied.

"Yes, the *'Ifs'* in life. Hmm. You really like Lorna, don't you?"

"Oh yes, our age difference doesn't matter, she's become a good friend. She has a very interesting history and has gone through a lot." I sighed for a moment. "Did you know that she wrote copious notes from the journals and letters before she made the tapes? She gave me her notebooks."

"She was a teacher, Sar. I guess that shows."

"She thinks I should discuss all this with Dad."

"I agree with her. What's holding you back?"

"Well, he's still pretty fragile and has bad days since Mom passed away. We all miss her, especially as she died so suddenly and unexpectedly. I sometimes still can't believe it. You must have felt that way after losing both your parents."

"Yes, I still do some days. But my parents died together, so I don't know what it must be like for one of them to live without their partner after a long life together."

"Even after someone dies their pearl doesn't fall off your string. It must be quite an adjustment for Dad to be single again after being married for so many years. Their group is ardent bridge players, but now he feels like the odd man out. He told me that he thinks he reminds them of their mortality. Mom was a healthy woman, but the doctors in Florida said she could have had that aneurysm for years, and then one day it just burst. That could happen to anyone, and age isn't necessarily a factor, but Mom was the first of their group to pass away, so I think it was a bit of a sobering experience."

"Do you remember that night at *Frogs* when Lorna and Dad were both there, at the end of the school year?" Ro nodded. "Well, she told Dad that she plays bridge at the senior center, and he has gone a few times."

"Really?" Her eyebrows shot up in surprise.

"They pick numbers or something to decide who plays at each table. Dad has anonymity there, and no one thinks of him as being half of the Rauf and Diane unit, so he feels comfortable. They have coffee after the game, so there is a social element to it, as well. I like his friends and I know they are doing everything they can to help him, but I also think it's a good thing that he is getting out on his own and meeting new people. Lorna told him that she went through the same thing when her husband died, so she can relate to that."

"Do you think that he and Lorna…?"

"Oh no, nothing like that. They don't go to the center together. She just mentioned it to him, and he has turned up a few times. It is way too soon for Dad, and I don't think Lorna is thinking of him as an eligible widower. Dad has had a lot of changes in the past year, and she is helping him to navigate his way. He not only has to reinvent himself as a retiree but a single one at that. The fact that they know each other may be advantageous to me, though."

"How so?"

"Well, Dad is a very private person, and we don't know what he knows. It is possible he doesn't even know he had a brother. He may not be too pleased to learn that Lorna is aware of all this family history because she did the translation. It may be helpful now that he's gotten to know her a bit."

We sat in silence again for a bit, watching the fireflies dancing around. A cloud cover moved to reveal a half-moon and a sky full of stars. We were both getting drowsy after a day in the sun and drinking wine for a few hours.

"Speaking of relationships, how are things with you and Ben?"

"Ben is great, Sarah, and not the pushy type at all. He and Joey get along well, and Joey likes him a lot. Ben is very independent and doesn't mind that I like my independence too."

"He does travel a fair bit, doesn't he?"

"Yes, he would always go to wherever the jobs were and often spent months in some remote area building a bridge or dam or whatever. He'll be forty soon, and never married probably because he didn't stay in one place long enough."

"Do you think he wants to get married?"

"Now that he has his own business, his focus is on cultivating new projects. He wants to keep his headquarters in Toronto and hire a foreman and crew for the hands-on part wherever the job may be. That's what he's doing in Alberta right now."

"You could travel with him. That's something you've always wanted to do," I suggested. "Do *you* think about marriage?"

"I don't know, Sarah. Joey has always been my main focus, but he's eight years old now. When I thought he was lost or hurt the other day I completely panicked. I don't know what I would do if I lost him." She sighed. "I can't believe where those years have gone, but the reality is that before I know it, he will be a young man and ready to have his own life. I want that for him, and I'll have to let him go to become the man he is meant to be, but it won't be easy. Then I'll be a middle-aged woman with a rocking chair and a cat."

"Hey, I live with a cat."

"Zipper isn't really a cat, is he? I thought he was your roommate." We both laughed.

"Maybe you and Joey could travel with Ben. You could always homeschool Joey if you were going to be away for any length of time. Joey is very resilient, and it would be a great learning experience for him."

"Ben gave Joey a Lego set for his birthday and that's all he plays with these days. One night he and Ben were building something, and Ben was explaining how to reinforce the building from the bottom to give it stability. Joey questioned Ben about it and in the end, agreed it made sense. Geez, they sounded like two engineers discussing a problem."

"Joey is so smart."

Ro looked at me with a deadpan expression and said, "You see it too, don't you?"

We laughed again.

"Joey is still so young, though, Sarah. I don't know what will happen, but I guess you can't hold back time. He will grow up, and I will still have a life to live. What about you, though, Sar? You've been on your own for a few years. Do you ever think about getting married again?"

"Never say never, but I guess fate would play a role, too. You met Ben in the supermarket; maybe something unexpected will happen to me, too."

We sat for a while, listening to the sounds of the lake. A loon cried in the distance.

Two young healthy women with tanned legs and pedicured toes; independent lives, careers, assets, and minds of our own. In charge of our own destinies and not settling for less than what we want in our lives.

Chapter Eighteen

MY DAD

DAD ALWAYS ENJOYED manning the barbeque but didn't have much opportunity to do so since moving to the condo. I invited him over to grill steaks in my backyard. I set up a table on my small patio where I knew we would have privacy.

He seemed relaxed and we enjoyed some light conversation while we ate. Zipper appeared through the hedge, ate his dinner by the back door, and then settled in a patch of late-day sunlight that filtered through the maple tree.

"That was great, Sarah. I can't remember when I last barbequed."

I moved our dishes into the kitchen and came back with a tray of coffee and a bottle of Amaretto, Dad's favourite.

"This is nice," he said while he poured coffee for both of us and added a splash of liquor. "What are we celebrating?"

"Well, there is something I want to talk to you about." I sipped my liquor-based coffee for courage while my heart pounded a bit faster in my chest.

He looked at me quizzically, took out his pipe, and settled into his ritual. I plunged in and I told him everything. His expression changed often, but he did not interrupt me.

"Did you know about all this, Dad?" I asked.

He didn't say anything for a few minutes and then asked if he could see the box. When I came back and placed it on the table, he was pacing around the patio. It was dusk by now and the light was fading so his face was hidden in shadows.

He touched the box but didn't open it.

"You say this box was hidden in your mother's sewing room?"

"Yes, in that funny closet with the step up."

"I lived in that house for most of my life, but I could probably count the number of times I was in that room."

He touched the box again and this time he opened the lid and took out one of the journals.

"This is written in German, Sarah, how were you able to read it?"

"Well, I wasn't. I had someone translate it for me." I knew I was on thin ice. My parents were not the type to yell when we were growing up, but they each had an expression that spoke volumes. He wore his now as he looked at me.

"Why didn't you tell me about this, Sarah?"

"You and Mom were on that cruise when the box was delivered to my office. Adele, the real estate agent, got it from the new owners of the house and she knew you had authorized me to deal with anything that came up from the sale."

"Given the fact that this information was obviously hidden away, didn't make you think that perhaps it was of a personal nature?"

Fortunately, he did not ask me if the box had been locked and I did not volunteer that I had broken into it. "You could have called me in Florida when we returned from the cruise."

"You are right, Dad, I should have called you. But after learning the contents of the first journal, I felt it would be better to speak to you about it in person. I wanted to wait until you had returned from Florida, but then everything happened with Mom, and it got lost in the confusion."

"So, you went ahead and had all the journals translated?" He lifted the other journals but did not take them out of the box. "And the letters?"

I nodded.

"Who translated them for you?" I knew by the tone of his voice that he was angry, and my heart sank.

"Lorna."

"Lorna? The woman you introduced me to?"

"Yes, Dad. She is a good friend. She was raised in Germany and is bilingual."

He raised his head, and I could see that he was deeply hurt. He turned away without saying anything.

"Dad, the information in those journals is amazing. Grandma was a wonderful woman and I'm glad that I know her history. I had no idea what she went through, and I can't tell you how much I admire her. Lorna felt the same way. The translation is on tapes in the box if you want to take it with you."

He closed the lid and said, "No, I do not want to do that."

He walked to the driveway, got into his car, and drove away without another word. Zipper curled around my legs and meowed as he looked up at me. I picked him up and held him close.

I was devastated at the way things had gone with my dad. I tried calling him the next day and for several days after, but he didn't pick up, or if he did, he was evasive and silent.

Lorna dropped in to see me one night. Ro had told her what had happened, but I had evaded talking to her, knowing she would be upset, too.

"Sarah, I'm so sorry it worked out this way. I feel responsible for encouraging you to talk to your dad."

"I knew you would feel that way, Lorna, but the responsibility is all mine. And I handled it so badly. I should have known it was too soon to talk to him."

We were sitting on the front porch and Zipper was curled up on my lap. He had stuck close to me all week; don't ever believe that animals aren't intuitive and don't absorb your feelings. They know when you are sad or troubled.

"He is still grieving for my mom, and to throw the origins of his background into the mix was extremely insensitive on my part. I told him how proud I am of my grandmother and her history, but it has added to his grief. How could I be so stupid?"

"Sarah, I think you were excited and impressed with what we learned and wanted to share that with him. I think he will come around."

John and Dana got married on Labour Day weekend and everyone was there except Ian. He had sprained his ankle playing racquetball, and his leg was in a cast. Kate said he couldn't very well show up in a suit jacket and a pair of shorts, hobbling around on crutches. She brought Lorna as her guest.

We caught a few quiet moments during the reception and Lorna inquired about Dad. I told her things had not changed, and if anything, he was even more withdrawn. She asked if she could talk to him, but I said no.

"Lorna, I don't want you to feel bad. I solicited your help and I appreciate your concern now, but I don't want you to worry about it."

The following weeks were tenuous and difficult. Ro was a steadfast and supportive friend, but I felt weary and adrift. My friends wondered about the change in my demeanour, but Ro ran interference and told them I was dealing with something personal. I spent time at home with Zipper or walking on the beach. I wanted to talk to my brothers but instinctively felt that Dave, being a lot like Dad, would probably be upset with me. One night I called Mike and told him I really wanted to see him.

He invited me for Thanksgiving weekend. I flew to Montreal on Saturday and Marc prepared a wonderful dinner for us. After dinner, we retired to the living room area with coffee.

"All right, Sarah, what's going on? What's happened?"

"It's about Dad. It's something I did that has really rocked the boat."

"Do you want me to leave the room, Sarah?" Marc asked. "Is this a family matter?"

"Yes, it's a family matter but you are family and I want you to stay."

Over the next few hours, I told them about our grandmother. They peppered questions along the way, which I answered to the best of my knowledge about her life.

"Wow, she was some kind of brave," said Marc at one point.

"I never would have suspected any of this when we were growing up, Sarah. Did you?"

I shook my head.

"Does Dad know about this?"

"That's the problem, Mike. I told him about it, but he took it very hard, and he refuses to talk about it. He was just starting to come out of his funk, but now he seems more depressed than ever. And it's my fault. I don't know if he feels betrayed that he didn't know his own history, or if he buried it all these years ago and doesn't want to be reminded of it. In any case, he feels I went behind his back by delving into it without his knowledge."

"I see what he means in a way, but that's how Dad is, Sarah. The ostrich syndrome. He can be stubborn, and things he doesn't want to acknowledge get buried. But for the record, I think you must have inherited some of Grandma's bravery."

I laughed. "What do I do about it now?"

Marc left early Sunday morning for the restaurant. They were booked solid for Thanksgiving dinner and there was a lot of preparation that needed to be done.

Mike and I were in the kitchen drinking coffee when the phone rang. Mike mouthed that it was Marc.

"He wants to know what time your flight leaves tomorrow."

"I'm booked on the 10:00 am Air Canada shuttle."

He relayed this information to Marc and hung up with a shrug. A half-hour later the phone rang again.

"What— Marc, wait— " He hung up. "Marc booked me on your flight. He wants me to go with you tomorrow to talk to Dad."

Hours later Marc came home exhausted from his long day. I went straight into his arms and gave him a huge hug. Mike and I had walked for hours that afternoon all over Montreal. It was a crisp day with autumn in the air, and it did us both good. We talked about everything and became friends as well as siblings.

I had my car at the airport in Toronto and we drove straight to Dad's condo the following day. He was dumbfounded to find us at his door. Mike took the lead; I had never seen him like that before. He said the revelations regarding our family history left him gratified that we had a grandmother like ours. He went on in this manner for some time, glossing over my misguided handling of the matter. He also asked Dad if he had known any of it.

"I was aware of some parts of the story," Dad replied but did not elaborate.

No one said anything for a few minutes. We had hoped Dad would say more, but when he didn't, Mike stood up and paced the room.

"There's something else that I've wanted to talk to you about for some time Dad. I'm gay. It's who I am. It has nothing to do with you and Mom; it's the way I've always been. And I'm glad that I'm gay because it brought Marc into my life. He's my life partner, Dad, and I'm lucky to have such a loving and supportive person to share my life."

I hadn't said much but spoke up then. "Marc is a great guy, Dad. In fact, he booked Mike on my flight this morning to come and talk to you."

"You were in Montreal?"

I nodded.

"So, you went there to discuss all this with Mike and Marc?"

I nodded again.

"Well, you two have certainly gone to a lot of trouble to bring up things that were probably better left unsaid."

I drove Mike back to the airport, but we had about an hour before his flight, so we decided to grab a sandwich in one of the restaurants. He looked lighter to me somehow.

"I'm glad we did this, Sarah. Don't feel so bad, I think Dad will come around—at least about the grandma part. I don't know if he will ever accept my lifestyle but I'm glad it is out in the open. You can't know how many times I've wanted to do that; I'm just sorry that I didn't do it while Mom was still alive."

"You are lucky to have someone like Marc in your life. I love you Mike, and I'm glad that you're happy. Thank Marc for everything and give him a big squeeze for me."

He reached out and took my hand. "I love you, too. Knowing about Grandma's history means a lot to me and so do you. Please stay in touch and come to Montreal anytime."

I didn't hear from Dad until mid-November. He called me at work to say he was leaving for Florida. He and the Henderson's were travelling in tandem so he wouldn't have to be on the road alone. He had his mail redirected to Florida but asked me to check on his condo occasionally over the winter. He said he would drop the keys off at my office.

Christmas came—our first without Mom, but we were all in different places. Mike told me he had 'come out' to Dave in a phone call and had briefed him about the rift with Dad. Dave called me to say they were spending Christmas with Sherri's family and halfheartedly invited me to join them. He seemed relieved when I declined. Nothing more was said.

My friends made sure I was busy over the Christmas season, and I accepted all invitations but had a hard time getting into the spirit of things. The New Year brought some good news, though. I was promoted to the position of Senior Manager, which was a boost to my morale. At least my professional life was on track. We had a celebration at *Frogs* with my friends making a big deal of how I was out of their league and making me promise to remember them as I climbed the corporate ladder. I laughed more that night than I had in months. Lorna was there and told us she and Margery were renting a condo in Florida for the month of February. They were flying and renting a car for the duration of their stay.

January passed in a flurry of settling into my new role. Keeping busy was the perfect energizer and my mood lifted tremendously. I collected my messages from reception one day in early February and was alarmed to find one from Dad.

"I'm glad you called me back so quickly, Sarah," Dad said. "No, no everything is fine here. I, um, just wondered if you would be able to come visit me in Florida I'd really like to see you."

"Of course, Dad. I can come on the weekend if you like."

"It would be nice if you could stay for a few days. Let me know the details of your flight and I'll pick you up at the airport."

I arranged for a few days off and called Mike to tell him what I was doing.

"Progress, Sarah. Let us know how it works out. Love you."

Chapter Nineteen

FLORIDA

I HAD BEEN in the house in Florida the previous year when Mom passed away but didn't remember much about it. We sat in the sunroom, and I noticed how nice everything looked. The weather was great, and the community was in full bloom.

Dad seemed a bit fidgety as he poured drinks for us. We made small talk, but he looked as though he was expecting someone. When a car pulled into the driveway, he jumped up and went to the door.

"Lorna?" She walked into the sunroom and gave me a big hug.

"I'll fix us drinks," Dad said picking up our glasses and disappearing into the kitchen.

I started to ask her what was happening, but she motioned me to be quiet. "Let your dad do this his way."

"I guess you're surprised to see Lorna here."

I nodded looking from one to the other.

"She showed up unexpectedly last week and well, basically told me off. She said if I didn't get over myself, I could lose you kids forever. I wasn't too happy about being confronted like that at first, but we started talking and I calmed down. One thing led to another, and we ended up talking the whole thing out."

"Dad, I…."

"Let me finish Sarah. I'm still not thrilled about how this evolved, but I've been thinking a lot about your grandmother and her life. There is a lot about what you've uncovered that I didn't know, but let's start with what I did know."

"Your mother and I needed birth certificates to obtain a marriage license. I thought it was a simple request to ask your grandmother for my birth certificate, but it caused her a great deal of distress, which I didn't understand at the time. Days went by, and time was getting short. Our wedding date had been set, and I needed that information. Finally, she told me the short version of her first marriage in New Jersey, how my father had died of the Spanish flu, her marriage to William, and how they came to live in Toronto. But the bigger issue was that William had not adopted me, which created another problem. I had no legal right to the name Langner, so I had to hire a lawyer and get my name changed. All of this had to be done in a great hurry."

"So, we are really Meyers and not Langners?"

"Legally we are Langners. I thought about Meyer as being my birth name, but it was all so confusing and would have created more problems if I had insisted on using it. But I was angry at both William and your grandmother. I was twenty-six years old and about to be married. I felt I had the right to know about her previous marriage and my background. I didn't even know I had been born in New Jersey. I assumed that they had emigrated from Germany directly to Canada. Your grandmother told me she had planned to explain all this to me someday, but perhaps she thought it would just never come up."

"After your mother and I were married, and the dust settled, I got the idea of moving to the United States, possibly California, as I was actually an American citizen. Your mother wasn't as keen on the idea, but I was all fired up about it. Dave was born in our first year of marriage and he was just a toddler when we were expecting Mike. Those first few years were difficult for your mother, but to her credit, she was patient with me. I was angry and can be set in my ways when I think I'm right."

I did the eye roll and Lorna smiled behind her glass at that comment.

"I've never known you to be an angry man, Dad."

"That's because I learned early in life to suppress my anger. Getting angry at William was useless because he did not react in any way. Trying to win his approval was a lost cause, too. I grew up thinking that I would never measure up to him, as hard as I tried."

"Your mother and I talked about moving for many months, but then another shift occurred. Your grandmother would light up like a Christmas tree whenever she saw the boys. I started to realize how empty her life was with William, and that my family gave her life meaning. When you were born, she was elated to have a little girl to fuss over."

I smiled at my memories. "What about your relationship with William? It must have been difficult to continue to work for him."

"Actually, it became easier; knowing that I wasn't his son said a lot about our relationship and removed some of the guilt that I felt about him. My self-esteem improved, and I became interested in the business. I learned everything I could about manufacturing and implemented changes which I would like to believe kept the business viable for many years. William was getting older and slowly released his grip on the business. Years later, when imports started to take over the market in Canada, I knew it was the right time to let it go. And the education I had from operating it all those years enabled me to start my consulting business."

He paused for a moment lost in thought, then said, "Let me refresh our drinks."

I looked wide-eyed at Lorna, but she just shook her head. Dad came back with our drinks and continued.

"There was a lot I didn't know about your grandmother, as it turns out. I didn't know about her being a maid in the Koenig household or how she met my paternal father; her journey to America and the Italian family that took her in. But the biggest shock was discovering that I had a brother." He paused and took a deep breath.

"I've been thinking about that a lot over these past months and some memories have surfaced. I faintly remember that trip to Germany when I was about twelve. We only spent an afternoon in Wernigerode, and I knew the people were related to us, but I was somewhat bored by the whole experience. Everyone was speaking German and I have a rudimentary knowledge of the spoken language, but the conversation didn't interest me. We visited a farm on the way back to *Hamburg,* and I do recall a young boy that I believe must have been Erik. He was older than me but slight in stature and seemed very backward and shy. Your grandmother tried to draw him out, I think, but he was awkward and didn't engage at all. She was quite silent and withdrawn for a few days afterward, but that didn't mean a lot to me at the time."

"Discovering that William had coerced your grandmother into marrying him for the money that had been meant for Erik appalled me, at first, but knowing that she helped her family in the best way she could, has made me realize that she was made of stronger stuff than I realized."

"You never knew that she sent money and supplies to Germany in those years?"

"No, and I doubt that William did either. We were in the factory for long hours every day, so she was able to do that in secrecy." He sighed. "Knowing what I know now I'm glad that I didn't abandon her all those years ago."

Dad seemed to have run out of steam and Lorna rose to leave. We walked her to her car and impulsively Dad asked if he could take all of us for dinner the following evening. Lorna said she would talk to Margery but accepted the invitation.

He and I spent time talking over the next few days while I was in Florida. I knew I had to tread lightly and let him deal with this at his own speed. I realized that in my zeal to uncover this story I had ignored the fact that this was his life we were talking about. I knew who I was and where I had come from, but he was being bombarded with information that undermined most of what he thought he knew about himself.

I was also discovering things about him that came as a surprise to me. On the last evening of that trip, we took a long walk on the beach after dinner. It was a balmy evening, and we watched the sunset while I gathered stones as we walked in silence. I so wanted to know him as the boy and young man he had been. I realized that his stony silences when we were growing up were his way of suppressing the anger he must have felt at some of the shenanigans we had gotten up to as children. I wondered if yelling might have been better, if we may have learned to express our own feelings, rather than fear of disappointing him. I recognized these traits in the way Dave was raising his children and of course Mike's reluctance to reveal his lifestyle. Grief for my mother washed over me. I missed her terribly and wished she were here to help me understand this man she had loved for so many years.

Dad broke the silence. "Do you think Mike would come for a visit?" he asked.

I smiled at this man who was trying so hard to break through the walls he had built over a lifetime. "I love you, Dad."

Chapter Twenty

THE TAPES

THE FIRST ANNIVERSARY of my mother's passing occurred while Dad was in Florida. My brothers and I didn't know how to handle it, but Dad resolved the matter by calling each of us on that day. We didn't make it a sad conversation, but rather more of a reconnecting as a family.

When he returned from Florida, things slowly went back to normal. We started having our weekly dinners again and he returned to playing bridge at the senior's center. One evening he asked to see the box. He didn't want to discuss it with me but said he'd like to take it home with him. I showed him the gold wedding ring in the velvet bag and indicated that I would like to have it. He turned it over in his hand and placed it back in the bag. He looked pensive but agreed and placed it in my hand.

I tentatively mentioned that I felt the story wasn't quite finished and wanted to do more research on the cast of characters in my grandmother's story. He didn't say much about it but also did not object, so I took that as his way of agreeing with me. I wanted to be completely transparent with him on the subject.

I had given Lorna the tape recorder when she agreed to do the translating as a convenience to her. I felt it would be less cumbersome than having to write out the translation. I realized later that the audio version of the story was much more compelling than a transcript would have been. Lorna had a way of channelling my grandmother through the telling, in a very poignant way. She was pragmatic and didn't embellish or detract from the story but told it in a way that my grandmother may have done herself.

Ro and I both commented that while listening to the tapes and knowing Lorna's own tale of leaving her parents behind at the start of WWII, we found empathy in her voice regarding the realities of those times. Lorna is a poised and classy woman, and her way of speaking reflects that, but she is also approachable and intelligent with a genuine sense of humour.

Dad is not a cat person by nature, but when he would come for dinner, Zipper would often jump up on his lap. He had a calming effect on Dad, and he would sometimes unwrap a bit while stroking Zipper's soft coat. He mentioned playing bridge with Lorna and a few times they had gone on to dinner after the game. While my grandmother's story was tragic and unique to him, he began to acknowledge that thousands of families had undergone terrible circumstances during periods of war and pandemic. He found companionship and common ground with Lorna as they got to know each other.

One evening he said to me, "I've been seeing quite a bit of Lorna lately."

"I know Dad."

"Sarah, your mother—"

"Dad, Lorna is a lovely lady. I like her a lot and she has become a good friend. We miss Mom and always will, but I don't think she would want you to become a grumpy old man shuffling around in your bathrobe."

He laughed. "No, I don't suppose she would."

"Lorna misses her husband, too. She has a way of expressing herself calmly and matter-of-factly; you know she has suffered losses, but she is still young and making the most of her life."

With that comment, I knew that Dad had listened to the tapes, even if he hadn't said as much and that he appreciated the strength he found in Lorna. He didn't say anything about her visit to Florida, but I got the impression that in his own way he was glad she had confronted him.

I continued my quest to unravel the lives of my grandmother's family as well as the Meyers but suffered difficulties in knowing where to begin. I stumbled around the library a few times without much success until one of the librarians came to my rescue. She tried a few resources, but we came up empty. A week or so later she called to say she had found a recent publication out of Germany about the history of shipbuilding in that country. It was a coffee table book, so the library did not carry it, but she gave me the name of the publishing house. She also suggested that a genealogy group may be the place to start and gave me the name of someone she had found in *Hamburg*, Robert Schneider, who headed up such a group.

I wrote to the publishing house in Germany and obtained a copy of the book and sent a note to the genealogy group in *Hamburg*. The book was a wonderful publication with numerous pictures of ships through the ages. It featured the Koenig family, starting with the originator of the business in 1885, Albert Koenig. It appears that Albert is the Herr Koenig of my grandmother's time. His son Christian (the young boy that taught my grandmother to read, write, and play the piano), took over the business in 1928 when Albert fell into poor health. Christian went on to operate the business and kept it functioning through the Depression. His son Joerg, now retired, was next in line and the current President and CEO is his son Christian, named for his grandfather.

The helpful librarian named Cheryl told me that many people are interested in genealogy. But the hardcore genealogists are usually older people, often retired, who have the interest and time to do the research. Robert Schneider was such a person and his response to my note was interesting. He wrote that births, marriages, and deaths were often recorded in family bibles or churches in small communities, many of which had been lost during wartime. But he encouraged me not to give up and included a list of the members of his group. My eye immediately caught the name of Joerg Koenig, complete with an address in *Hamburg*.

I wrote to Joerg Koenig, telling him about my grandmother, and asked if he could provide any information about her. He responded that they often did not know much about the people in their household employ during those years, but he would see if he could find anything. I also mentioned the Meyer family but did not go into detail about my interest in that regard.

Joerg and I wrote back and forth a few times and I kept Dad apprised of my findings. He read Joerg's letters and the coffee table book where the Koenig family was featured. In late spring, I told Dad I wanted to take a trip to Germany and asked him to go with me.

"You are really intrigued by all this, Sarah, aren't you?" Ro asked one afternoon as we walked on the beach.

"Yes, I am. I can't explain it, but I don't think the story is finished. I'm drawn to the idea of visiting the place of my ancestors, and I'd also like to see some of Germany."

"Do you think your dad will go with you?"

"He's thinking about it."

PART TWO

Chapter Twenty-One

THE KOENIG FAMILY

DAD AND I arrived in Hamburg on a Sunday morning in early August after a direct overnight flight from Toronto. We wanted the European experience, and our travel agent did not disappoint. She booked us into a two-bedroom suite on the fourth (top) floor in a charming boutique hotel, in a mid-town section of the city. The building was nestled in an area that promised shops, restaurants, and cafes within easy walking distance. There was a sitting room with comfortable high-back wing chairs, ottomans, and an antique desk overlooking a courtyard through a huge window facing the back of the building. A small efficiency kitchen to the left revealed a coffee maker with pouches of coffee, a kettle for tea, and a cupboard with China dishes including cups and saucers, cutlery, wine, and water glasses. There was a small fridge stocked with ice, cream for coffee, and bottled water. To the right were two bedrooms comfortably appointed with double beds, closets, a bureau for folded clothes, luggage racks, and a wing-back chair in each. A bathroom was accessible to each of the bedrooms. The façade of the building looked like it had been there for years, but the suite was spacious and clean, decorated in relaxing colours and decked out with modern features.

Dad and I decided on a walk, but found the shops closed, as it was Sunday. Despite this, they offered interesting window shopping and we vowed to explore them on another day. We did find a grocery store that was open where we picked up pastries, cheese, and fruit that would provide us with a leisurely breakfast in our suite. I noticed wine in the grocery store and added a bottle to our stock. Back in the hotel we spotted pamphlets offering city tours and stopped at Reception to book one for the following morning. We mentioned that we wanted to go to Munich for a few days the following week, and the Receptionist offered to book rail tickets and a hotel for us. All in all, we were very pleased with everything so far.

Convincing my dad to take this trip with me had not been easy. I was determined to go, and I really wanted to meet Joerg Koenig. I felt he could give us some direction from a genealogy perspective, but curiosity about the family my grandmother worked for, was the guiding light for me. I think Dad may have felt the same, although he never said as much. Dad had mellowed considerably in the past few years, but he was from a different era. He had come to accept that I was divorced and his son was gay, but it was hard for him. Revealing his mother's history had been a tough nut for him to swallow.

Lorna played an important role in Dad's metamorphosis, but she did so in an unobtrusive way. Their relationship evolved over the months. They had a lot in common, and after a while, it was accepted by both family and friends that they would turn up together at events. My friendship with Lorna deepened; she and I shared a special bond, and I was grateful to her not only for taking the journey through my grandmother's life with me but also for being instrumental in healing my fractured relationship with Dad. It was Lorna who broke the ice in Florida and helped break down the barriers. I was also convinced that she influenced Dad to come to Germany with me.

I was enthusiastic about meeting Joerg Koenig, although Dad was a bit more reserved. I may have convinced him that Joerg, being two generations away from my grandmother's time, could be a good resource for us, but probably would not know of our relationship with the Meyer family. Dad was adamant that it remained that way.

When we returned to our suite, Dad decided to take a nap and I placed a phone call to Joerg Koenig. We had corresponded over the previous months and when he learned we were coming to Hamburg, he replied that we should visit him. We had a chat about our trip and he invited us for coffee the following afternoon.

On Monday morning, we took a city tour of Hamburg and decided we liked the city very much. The mix of old and new architecture speaks of yesterday and today. Being a port city, Hamburg attracts tourists and commerce from all over the world and has many cultural and entertainment opportunities. We also took note of the Municipal buildings and a huge library where we planned to research while we were there. Dad did not want to mention the Meyer family or our connection to it when we visited Joerg, but we hoped to do some digging on our own.

A taxi took us to Joerg's address in Altstadt, one of the oldest residential areas in Hamburg. The homes in this area have retained their old-world charm with beautifully kept properties and gardens full of colour. A woman answered the door of a stunning vintage three-storey home and introduced herself as Marta. As we followed her down the hall to the back of the house, we noticed gleaming hardwood floors and area carpets complimenting wainscoting on the walls. There were ships everywhere—in pictures on the walls and replicas on tables, even a huge sailboat on the mantel above the fireplace in the living room. Marta led us to a study next to a large kitchen. Joerg was sitting in a leather wing chair beside French doors open to the garden.

He greeted us warmly, but we could see he was not in good health. His hands were gnarled with arthritis, and it was an effort for him to stand, but he was an attractive man with a pleasant demeanour and lively eyes that shone with intelligence. He welcomed us to make ourselves comfortable while Marta went to the kitchen to prepare coffee.

We thanked him for the invitation and complimented him on his beautiful home.

"The house belongs to my son, Christian," he said. "He bought it after his divorce a few years ago. I was living alone since his mother passed, so he invited me to join him here. My rooms are on the second floor, but this is where I spend my time. I enjoy looking over the garden and watching the birds."

"Does Christian operate the shipping business now?" Dad asked.

"Oh yes, and that boy works too hard. He rarely takes time off, except when my grandson Julien is here."

Marta brought coffee and cake.

The study was lined with shelves filled with leather-bound books, and there was an attractive chess set on a side table. We chatted amiably over coffee. Joerg said that his interest in genealogy started when he was approached to contribute to the coffee table book and was pleased when we told him we had acquired a copy of it. A couple of hours passed, and we had not yet broached the topic of my grandmother's time in the Koenig home when Christian arrived. Introductions were made and he offered drinks.

Joerg invited us to stay for dinner. Marta had left and we did not want to impose, but Christian said he would order dinner, and went to the telephone to make the arrangements.

Over dinner, we discussed the Koenig genealogy. Albert had started the business in 1885 and his son Christian propelled it through the depression years of the 1930s. Joerg took over during the turmoil of World War II and the reconstruction of Germany, and the present-day Christian was now converting the shipping line to passenger and cargo carriers.

Dad asked if his son would continue the business one day. Christian laughed and said that Julien is an electronics wizard and wants to computerize everything.

The only other living relative is Hannah, the granddaughter of Julia (the young girl under my grandmother's care). Both Joerg and Christian smiled at the mention of her name.

"Hannah is a talented designer and has done the restoration and redesign of the Koenig house, which is now the Koenig Inn. We all lived there at one time or another, but the house and grounds are too big for us now. However, it was the perfect size for a small Inn. She has a design company and a boutique where she retails her own furniture and fixtures. She is well known in the design community, but she is quite eccentric and has no head for business." He laughed again. "Her sense of detail in design is flawless, but she needs help in the financial end of things."

He told us more about the Inn. "It has six rooms for overnight guests. There were more bedrooms but some of that space has been taken up to add bathrooms on the second floor. The dining room is popular and frequently booked for events or business meetings. That is where our dinner tonight came from," he explained. We agreed that it has an excellent chef, as the meal had been delicious.

The subject finally turned to that of my grandmother. Joerg said that they did not have records of their employees from that long ago, but they may have some pictures. He would try to find them for us.

We said we wanted to go to Wernigerode, and to our surprise, Christian said he would take us there. He said he would enjoy a day out of the city and perhaps he could help deal with a Municipal office as the clerks in small villages were often not fluent in the English language. He had meetings the following day, but we arranged to make the trip on Wednesday.

Dad and I went to the library on Tuesday morning and combed through city directory archives for the Meyer Wallpaper Company. We did find a company of that name established in the late 1890s but lost the trail after World War One. The librarian suggested we look in the obituaries, but we did not know Herr Meyer's first name. We then asked about military records, as we knew Hans fought in the war, but Meyer is a common name and without a date of birth we had little to go on.

Christian pointed out various things along the way to Wernigerode the next day. We would not have had that experience if we had driven ourselves, so it was doubly pleasant to enjoy his company as well as learn these bits of information. He took us to the address in Greta's letters, but the streetscape was much different from the way my grandmother described it in their time.

Numerous small towns and villages in Europe have foot traffic only in the centers, so Christian parked the car, and we walked the cobblestone streets.

We found what appeared to be a Municipal office and Christian inquired about the Baehr family. He learned that there are numerous people with the Baehr name in the community, but their records did not go back as far as we wanted. He told us that two churches have been in the community for many years, but as this is prime farmland, they had been resting spots to eat and sleep in both wars for the soldiers marching through Germany. Unfortunately, destruction followed, and records were lost. There is an old cemetery on the edge of Wernigerode. Many of the graves, however, are unmarked and even those that had marks had faded over the years.

He suggested that we could ask around the village, but that did not seem hopeful. We did visit a few shops and stopped at a café for coffee, but no one had any useful information. We left Wernigerode disappointed, but not surprised. Dad and I wondered if one of the farms we passed had been Heinrichs' where Erik had spent most of his young life.

When Christian dropped us at our hotel, we accepted his invitation to have dinner on Friday night at the Koenig Inn.

Thursday found us at the library again, searching through obituaries from newspapers on microfiche. We thought if we found one for Herr Meyer it might name other family members, but it was tough going. The librarian said that a date of birth would be useful, as obituaries state the date of birth as well as death. Hours later, Dad and I were both going cross-eyed from paging through endless screens. The librarian told us that all major cities carried copies of international newspapers, so if we came across more information, we could try the library in Toronto, if their archives went back that far.

We needed to stretch our legs, so we went for a long walk, stopping here and there at shops that caught our attention. Our hotel had recommended a restaurant at the harbour, and we enjoyed dinner and a bottle of wine while overlooking the North Sea.

Christian picked us up in the late afternoon on Friday. The Koenig Inn is also located in Altstadt, not far from his home. It is a beautiful estate on a corner surrounded by manicured gardens enclosed by rod iron fencing. The building is brick and in places had an application known as '*Schmearing*,' which Christian explained is an old technique of using watered-down plaster where the brick had eroded. It suited the Inn and offered respect to its age.

There are high windows around the building with heavy casings, many of which had window boxes filled with colourful flowers and greenery. We noticed cement benches that looked like they had been there forever and wondered if they were the same ones my grandmother and Rauf had sat on to plan their future. A wide porch adorned the front of the Inn with comfortable chairs and small tables welcoming visitors. Christian explained that in good weather, they offer guests afternoon tea or pre-dinner cocktails on the porch. He suggested we take a quick tour of the Inn and enjoy a drink on the porch if that suited us. It was a balmy evening; I wore a flowered sundress with sandals and carried a light wrap. Dad decided on a sports jacket and tie and was glad to see that Christian was dressed similarly.

I had a huge lump in my throat as we entered through wide wooden doors and I could see that Dad had turned rather pale at the prospect of entering the home where my grandmother had experienced so much drama in her youth.

There was a room to our right that was once a bedroom but now served as a parlour with cozy chairs and a fireplace. A sweeping stairway led to the upper rooms that appeared to be original to the house but had been updated with new stain and stair runners. We entered the dining room on our left, which covered the entire side of the house. Christian said there had been a wall separating the original parlour and dining room, but it had been removed to offer a large dining room for dinners or meetings. We could see the flower boxes through the windows and a fireplace at both ends. This room was set up with elegant tables, crystals, and linens for dining. The kitchen was behind the stairway. As the chef and his staff were preparing the evening meal, we would not disturb them, but if we wanted to see the kitchen Christian promised he could arrange it for later. Dad and I looked at each other, both wondering about the small room that my grandmother had occupied during her day.

He settled us on the front porch and went back inside to order drinks. Dad and I were awestruck by the grandeur of the estate and our history with it. I gently took his hand, but neither of us spoke.

Christian returned with a waiter carrying a tray with our drinks. He mentioned that Hannah was joining us for dinner, and a few minutes later the most extravagant woman I have ever met arrived with a flourish. Everything about Hannah is extreme from her hair, makeup, clothing, jewelry, and mannerisms. Dad and I had been uneasy being in the house where seventy years earlier my grandmother had lived, worked, and ultimately undergone such life-changing events. But Hannah was so entertaining that we quickly got caught up in her personality. I noticed Christian's eyes crinkle as she kept up a flow of conversation all through dinner, but it was easy to see that he cared for her a great deal.

After dinner, she showed us one of the unoccupied guest rooms on the second floor and pointed out various works of art and décor that are reminiscent of the age of the house. She had tried to replicate the wallpaper, but told us it would have been very expensive to manufacture it in the way it had been in the days before the war. But the wall coverings were elegant and beautiful, and we decided she was indeed a talented designer.

The chef greeted us as we descended from the second floor and offered us a tour of the kitchen, inquiring if we had enjoyed our meals. It had been incredible, and we were happy to tell him how much we had enjoyed it. The kitchen had obviously undergone a complete renovation. It had state-of-the-art appliances, and everything a gourmet chef could need and was spotlessly clean. We did not see evidence of the small room where my grandmother had slept in this house, so it must have been incorporated into the redesign.

He offered us coffee and liquors and Christian led us to the small parlour at the front of the house where we settled into comfortable chairs. He may have noticed that Dad and I were rather overwhelmed by the whole experience but did not draw attention to it as Hannah kept up a steady stream of chatter. Later he took us to our hotel and said he was taking Julien sailing on Sunday and invited us to join him.

I had a very restless night, my dreams full of images of my grandmother in that exquisite house. Dad and I both slept in on Saturday morning and spent a quiet day. We wandered the nearby shops and picked up gifts for those at home, finally having a quiet dinner in a small café. We didn't talk much. I was still trying to absorb the events of the previous evening and felt sure that Dad was doing the same.

Chapter Twenty-Two

SAILING

IT WAS A good day for sailing. The water had a ripple to it and the wind was enough to keep us skimming along, but not so much that we felt we had to hold on for dear life. It was obvious that Christian and Julien are experienced sailors. Julien bears a strong resemblance to his father with his height, brown wavy hair, and hazel eyes they had both inherited from Joerg. Julien was a bit shy with us at first, but when he saw Dad fiddling with his camera, he went to take a look.

"This is a new camera, and I haven't got all the features figured out," Dad explained as he handed it to Julien.

"Be careful, Rauf, he may take it apart to see how it works," Christian remarked with a laugh.

They were on the starboard side of the sailboat while Christian and I were in the stern, with Christian at the helm and me sitting on a padded bench. I closed my eyes and raised my face to catch the sun and wind. I could hear Dad and Julien chatting over the camera.

I liked Christian. He was attractive, but not in a 'Hey, look at me' type of way that handsome men sometimes adopt. I like that he has taken on the patriarchal role in his family, taking care of Joerg, Julien, and even the effervescent Hannah. He is certainly generous, not only in extending hospitality to Dad and me, but also in asking us questions about our life in Toronto, appearing genuinely interested in what we had to say.

There is a sub-communication going on between us that I was thoroughly enjoying. It had been a long time since I felt this strong an attraction to a man. I opened my eyes and caught him smiling at me. I smiled back.

"I wish I had known how to use these features earlier in our trip," Dad said as he and Julien joined us. "I missed out on some good pictures, I think. Thanks for your help, Julien."

"You're welcome," he replied, then turned to Christian. "Dad I'm getting hungry."

They had brought a cooler on board and Julien opened it. It was filled with cheese, cold meat, bread, fruit, pastry, and cold drinks.

"Did you put this together?" I asked Christian.

Julien nodded. "Dad likes to cook. He is always asking the chef at the Inn for recipes. He makes great pizza."

Hmm, he even cooks, flashed through my mind.

We chatted comfortably as we enjoyed the snack, which was actually more of a meal. We were a fair distance out at sea, but sailing parallel to shore, shimming along with several other boats that were enjoying such a perfect day for sailing. After a while, we gathered up the wrappings and soda cans and put everything back in the cooler. Dad sat back on his bench and glanced over his shoulder at the expanse of the North Sea.

"This has certainly been a pleasure for us, Christian and Julien." He sighed, feeling relaxed. "I can only imagine what it must have been like for the first explorers who headed out to sea from ports like this. As pleasant as this is, it must have been terrifying for them."

"Yes, we are a seafaring family, but crossing the Atlantic can be difficult, even with our modern ships, especially at certain times of the year," Christian remarked. My thoughts went to my grandmother's journal—about her voyage to America and I shuddered a bit.

"Julien did a paper on the early explorers for school last year."

"Oh, that's interesting, Julien," Dad said. "Did you write about Christopher Columbus?"

"Not so much who, but more what their experiences must have been like."

"Christopher Columbus gets credit for discovering the Americas, but I've read that there were many before him," Dad said.

"The Vikings were probably among the first explorers," Julien started, "but they did not keep records in those early days. It could very well be that those explorers could not read or write, so only verbal accounts were kept. Those may have been lost or distorted in the telling. It's also possible that many of those ships never returned."

Dad nodded as Julien continued, warming to the subject. "There is a lot of controversy about Columbus. Was he Italian or Portuguese? We believe it is true that he was sponsored by Queen Isabella of Spain, but discovered Cuba before he landed in America. He may have been forced south, due to rough seas or navigation errors. A lot of navigation was by the stars and the moon and storms could easily have taken them off course.

My grandfather helped me with the research, and we found it really interesting. Many explorers were lost at sea due to drowning, of course, but there were so many other dangers they faced, especially the very early explorers. Everyone thought that sailing west would be a shortcut to Asia for trade, but they had no idea that the great mass of North and South America lay in their path. It must have taken a lot of courage to set sail to an unknown destination. They could have been at sea for months with no land in sight and no idea when or if they would find land."

Dad and I both involuntarily looked at the shore in the distance.

Julien grinned and continued. "Can you imagine the problems they would've faced? Did they have enough food and water for such long voyages? Also being stuck on a ship under harsh conditions, brutal discipline, and disease must have been unbearable. Even homesickness was an issue as many sailors were as young as ten or twelve years old. Psychologically it would have been impossible to bear with no end in sight.

Finding land, at last, would have been like waking from a nightmare, especially in the Caribbean, where the islands are so lush and beautiful. The people of those islands were welcoming and curious about the sailors, at least at first." Julien laughed, "It must have been quite something for those natives to see ships like that arrive with a crew of pale, thin, possibly deranged men on board. The natives were explorers too, and they travelled great distances in canoes, but to see ships like those and men in that condition would have been quite a culture shock. The explorers felt they had reached Utopia, no doubt. The natives made everything they needed from whatever was available on their islands, so when the explorers gifted them with metal dishes, utensils, and tools they were very intrigued. Offering gifts like that may have increased the welcome they received from the natives. Of course, the explorers were in no hurry to leave such an exquisite paradise where they had access to such bounty after the gruelling experience of being at sea for so long. Their health and spirits must have improved greatly."

"Use of the word 'bounty' reminds me of that movie," Dad said. "I can picture exactly what you are saying, Julien."

"Dad took us to the movie, as well," Julien said. "My grandfather said there was a lot of truth to it. Of course, it took place in the late seventeen hundreds when Europe and England had explored those waters pretty thoroughly, so they were better prepared for those voyages. Making it to the South Pacific was even more dangerous, though, as they had to cross Cape Horn which was famous for storms and rough seas.

But the bad news is that the majority of native people were wiped out by the white man's diseases such as the common cold and measles, which they had no defence against. Over many hundreds of years, Europeans settled in these places and claimed ownership."

"We have friends who went to Hawaii on vacation, and they learned a lot about the history," Dad said. "There are very few native Hawaiians left. Our friends attended a luau where they roasted a pig in the ground with banana leaves and ate poi and other native dishes. It was hosted by a Hawaiian family named Smith!"

Julien nodded. "Over time a lot of Europeans and English settled in the Americas and all over the Caribbean and Pacific. They either bought or just claimed these lands in the name of their home countries."

We continued this discussion for some time. Christian added a comment here and there, but for the most part, he seemed content to let Julien take the lead.

"I would love to read your paper, Julien," I said and Dad indicated his interest as well. "Have you considered becoming a Historian?"

"No, I'm more interested in communication and technology. History does intrigue me, though, when you think about how much progress has been made. The world is becoming a smaller place all the time."

"You are right about that," Dad said. "When I sold my business, the shoe manufacturing business, no one wanted the equipment. The equipment was antiquated years before the business was sold and there was no way we could keep up with the technology. The value was in the building."

He laughed. "One of the tenants that occupied space in the building after I sold it bought a few of our old sewing machines and made them into antique tables. I guess there was a market for that kind of thing. My value as a consultant in the manufacturing sector was based on my experience, but that's not to say I understand the type of equipment being used in new manufacturing."

"Dad, do you remember the old typewriter you gave me from the business?" He nodded. "When I was in high school, I decided it would be a good idea to learn how to type, so I practiced on that manual typewriter," I laughed. "If I wanted to make copies, I had to use carbon paper so making a mistake meant having to correct several copies by hand. It taught me to be careful."

"You learned how to type on a mechanical typewriter?" Julien asked. "How old are you, Sarah?"

"Julien!" Christian wasn't happy with that remark.

But I burst out laughing. Julien had the aptitude of a professor. Dad and I had thoroughly enjoyed our discussion with him and his intelligence over the previous hour or so, but in fact, he was a teenage boy. Still giggling, I touched Christian's arm to let him know I had not taken offence.

"If anything, Julien, you have proven your point. Look at the progress that has been made in the past twenty years. You are much smarter than I was when I was your age. Just think where you will be in the next twenty years."

The afternoon was starting to wane, and Christian decided we should head back to shore. Dad and I got out of the way while they came about and headed in that direction. We were leaving for Munich the next day and once underway, we talked about what Munich had to offer.

Julien was going to attend University there in a few years and was very excited about it. Christian suggested some places for us to see and was glad we were travelling by rail. He said we would see a lot more that way and would avoid the unpleasantness of the Autobahn.

We helped secure the ship at the dock and load the car with the cooler and other items we had taken on board. Dad was shaking Christian's hand, but I couldn't help but approach Julien and hug him, thanking him for such a nice day and reminding him that I wanted to read his paper. He coloured slightly but smiled and said he would get me a copy.

Dad shook hands with Julien, but I turned to Christian and found myself hugging him as well. It just seemed the thing to do but left me a bit unsteady on my feet. I blamed that on being on dry land after being on the ship for so many hours.

Chapter Twenty-Three

MUNICH

CHRISTIAN WAS RIGHT about the train. Dad and I were sun-kissed from being on the water the previous day, and it was relaxing and comfortable to just enjoy the ride. We sat facing each other with a table between us where we were served a light lunch. We were both amazed at the amount of farmland and vineyards, as we made our way south to Munich. Knowing the geographic size of Germany and its population we were amazed by the amount of open land.

Over coffee, Dad took out his pipe and tobacco pouch and began his ritual. I sat back and waited for him to speak.

"I'm glad we took this trip, Sarah, even though we didn't learn a lot about the Baehr family. Going to Wernigerode where my mother spent her youth was cathartic, I think."

I nodded. "Even though the area where they lived has changed, I don't think the village itself underwent any restoration. The buildings around the square appear to be originals. I can almost see it being the place where people gathered on market day, or after attending church on Sundays."

It was his turn to nod.

"And I'm glad we saw the Koenig Inn. It is such a stately and beautiful building."

"Yes, Hannah did a wonderful job of redecorating it, but I wonder what the original wallpaper was like?" I was picturing heavy flocked walls in all the rooms.

"Speaking of wallpaper, I've been thinking about the Meyer family. I don't see the point of continuing that search. I mean, even if we did find present-day members of that family, what purpose would it serve to contact them now? I've never felt like a Meyer, and it seems a bit redundant to seek out people I feel no connection to. It's very possible they wouldn't even know of my existence anyway."

He paused for a few moments as he fiddled with his pipe.

"It is logical to think the wallpaper business was named after the family, as most businesses were in those days. But we lost the thread after World War One in our research. We can only assume that the son Hans perished in the war, and with my father being out of the picture, there was no one to carry it on. We don't know what happened to Herr Meyer. The business may have collapsed after the war or when he died if there was no one to carry it on."

"It was interesting being in the Koenig Inn the other night. It's an ancient tale, Sarah, that young, naïve girls from the country go to work for wealthy families and are abused by the people who have the power to consider them dispensable. But I don't think that was the case in the Koenig household."

"I don't think so either, Dad. Grandma's story seems to indicate that Frau Koenig protected her. I felt her presence there, more than in Wernigerode, probably because she was older, and a lot more happened to her in that house."

"Perhaps Frau Koenig hoped that if my father learned he had sired a son, he would return to Germany and make amends with his father. Of course, the war intervened and changed all that."

"When Herr Meyer ordered her out of the house, I don't think she would have gone to the United States on her own."

"I've been thinking about that, too. The only other choice she had was to return to Wernigerode with Erik and of course, our fate would have been much different had she done that."

"You know, Dad, I feel Grandma was ahead of her time. Maybe I'm trying to read between the lines, but I think she had outgrown Wernigerode. Her experience in the Koenig house was different from Greta's, in that she welcomed the idea of being educated. She didn't appear to be content to have her father arrange a marriage with a cousin or neighbourhood boy and live the same life as everyone before her had."

"That may be so, Sarah, but in any case, she was certainly a strong woman to endure the trip to the United States and then lose my father so soon after. Ironically, she ended up with a marriage of convenience in the end anyway, with William." Dad sighed "Of course, the added tragedy to all this is Erik. There are so many ways this could have gone." He laughed slightly. "If my father had survived, they may have returned to Germany and again my fate, and yours would be rewritten. I have such a dim memory of Erik, but I do know that he was not a normal boy, so bringing him to America may have been too much for him."

"We have no way of knowing if he suffered trauma at birth or if the shock of everything that happened had an impact on his development. But Grandma never forgot him, or her family, and did what she could to help them against some tough odds. I admire and respect her. She certainly was a strong woman."

"I wonder if she would be pleased that we know her story," Dad said as he put his pipe back in his pocket.

A bit of a weight lifted in me at that, and I felt a new rapport with my father. Despite the way I had bungled the discovery of his ancestry, it appeared that this trip had helped to mend fences.

We sat in silence for a while watching the scenery slide by.

"The Koenig family has certainly treated us well. That sail yesterday was certainly a thrill. I didn't expect to experience anything like that on this trip. If that is an indication of the type of people they are, I am sure my mother did enjoy being in their home. Interestingly, they never inquired how our family ended up in Canada."

"Joerg's father, the first Christian, was a young boy in those years. He and his sister, Julia, spent time with Grandma, but after the war started things changed. I recall her journals stating that they had private tutors and were somewhere else in the house. The men had taken over the dining room and she and Cook were busy all the time in the kitchen, so she did not appear to see much of them. Albert Koenig did not know that Erik existed, so the children maybe didn't either, although that is hard to imagine. Joerg and Christen may have just assumed that Grandma married at some point and later emigrated to Canada."

"Well, it doesn't matter as I don't think we will see them again, but I certainly did enjoy meeting all of them. It might be nice to find some small gifts for them in Munich that we could send or drop off before we leave."

The thought of not seeing them again tugged at my heart a bit, but the reality was that we were leaving at the end of the week.

"That's a good idea, Dad."

Our hotel in Munich was in a busy area and our taxi ride from the train station gave us a glimpse of this thriving city.

Munich is another European city home to centuries-old buildings and numerous museums. The city is known for its annual *Oktoberfest* celebration and its beer halls, including the famed Hofbräuhaus, founded in 1589. We found our way to Marienplatz square with its popular glockenspiel show that chimes and re-enacts stories from the 16th century. As in Hamburg, the city also has modern buildings and crowds of people, which explains why there is so much open land in the countryside.

The following day we took a city tour and stopped to eat at a Biergarten. We sat at a long table with other tourists and locals. Anyone who thinks Germans are a stoic people has never visited a Biergarten. We laughed and chatted with these friendly people as we plowed through huge mugs of beer and schnitzel the size of a dinner plate, swearing we would never eat again.

On Tuesday we went shopping. We had purchased gifts for family and friends in Hamburg but added some additional items. Dad bought a beautiful silk scarf and chunky silver bracelet for Lorna. We ate lunch at an outdoor café, and I noticed a cavernous building across the courtyard, which appeared to be a shopping mall of sorts.

"Go ahead, Sarah," Dad said. "I'll have another cup of coffee and mind our bags here."

I found a bonanza of stores and indulged in purchases of clothing and shoes for myself. I realized I had been gone quite some time when I passed a window with a stunning dress suitable for a dinner out or special event. Wondering when I would ever have an occasion to wear something like that, I nevertheless tried it on and purchased it on the spot.

I was ready to apologize to Dad for being gone so long when I found him enjoying a glass of wine with a man about his age. He introduced him as Ed, an American tourist who had lost his wife in the bowels of the same mall.

"Did you happen to see a woman with her Visa card on fire in there?" Ed asked.

"Afraid not," I replied laughing, "I was too busy trying to keep mine from bursting into flame." I joined them in a glass of wine and when we left a half hour later, Ed was still waiting for his wife.

That evening Dad and I enjoyed a dinner theatre at our hotel, which included a delicious meal and a live comedy performance.

Our hotel in Hamburg held our suite for us for the next two nights. We were flying home to Toronto on Friday morning. When we returned from Munich, we found a message from Christian requesting we call him at his office. He said Joerg had found some pictures we might like to see and invited us to drop over that evening. We had gifts for them and so were delighted to accept his invitation.

We sat at the dining room table and Christian offered us coffee. We found an antique bird feeder for Joerg in a second-hand shop in Munich and he said he loved it and had just the right place for it in the garden. We spotted a ship in a bottle in the same shop for Christian. He frowned when he opened it and then his face broke out in a huge smile.

He showed it to Joerg and said, "Look, it's the Rickmer!"

Joerg leaned in to examine it more closely. "Why, so it is. Wherever did you find it?"

Christian explained that the Rickmer was built by one of the original shipbuilders in Germany and declared it a treasure. He clapped Dad on the shoulder and kissed me on the cheek, which elevated my heartbeat several notches.

Joerg cleared his throat and brought out the pictures he had found. There were formal portraits of that era of Albert and Anna, Christian and Marlis, and Joerg and Rebekka. There were also a few pictures of the exterior of the Koenig Inn, but the one that intrigued us the most was a shot of the dining room. Men were sitting around the table smoking cigars, and a young girl in a maid's uniform was serving coffee. The back of the picture was dated 1914 and it named the men, including Reinhold Meyer, so now we finally had his first name. We also knew that the young girl must have been Ava, my grandmother.

Dad and I gasped and studied the picture closely. Christian offered to have reprints made for us that he would send to me in Toronto. He also handed me a package stating it was a copy of the paper Julien had written. Later Joerg invited Dad to a game of chess in the study and Christian and I sat in the living room and chatted comfortably. He talked about his initiative of introducing passenger travel to what had always been cargo transport in their business. He had spent the past few years refitting one of the ships and had sailed to England and Spain with passengers. It had worked out well, and the company was beginning to attract passengers. The real test would be on a crossing to New York planned for September, about six weeks away.

It was clear that he was a risk taker, but cautiously so, and I admired him for it. I asked questions without being too intrusive about their business, and he appreciated my candour but also enjoyed debating some issues. I was thinking about how much I enjoyed his company and how this trip had been a revelation in so many ways.

After an hour or so, Dad said they had not finished their chess game, but Joerg was starting to tire. Christian settled him on the second floor and drove us to the hotel. He mentioned a new restaurant opening. The owner, Martin, was a good friend and had helped them hire chefs and staff for both the Koenig Inn and the ship. Martin was having a cocktail party the following evening to celebrate the opening and Christian invited us to join him. It would be our last night in Germany.

Dad and I took an excursion to Hamelin, the home of the Pied Piper, on Thursday. Hamelin is another interesting old village steeped in history. The legend of the Pied Piper originated here and dates back to the Middle Ages. Hamelin is another village with only foot traffic, so the bus parked, and the tour guide led us onto more cobblestone streets. She gave us time to look around in the shops and we had lunch in an outdoor café. Over lunch, a group of street performers enacted the story of the Pied Piper. The performers were primarily children and she explained that the schools in Hamelin and neighbouring villages sponsored these events every summer.

On the return to Hamburg, the tour stopped at a castle sitting high on a hill overlooking vast farmland. The tour guide explained that the castle had been built by stone masons and the land was worked by people under the care of the Duke or Earl, raising sheep and garden vegetables that fed them all. We toured the castle (which had a working moat) and wandered the grounds.

The land was still farmed, and we saw sheep grazing on the rolling hills and patches of garden vegetables.

When we returned to the hotel later that afternoon I went into my bedroom to pack. Dad made tea and settled himself into one of the wing chairs in the living room with a book. I poked my head out a bit later intending to ask him if he had room in his luggage for the overflow that I had acquired during my shopping trips but found him fast asleep in the chair. I smiled. It had been a busy trip with activity every day. I liked the way Dad looked in repose with his book in his lap, and not wanting to disturb him, I quietly went back into my bedroom to continue trying to squeeze my luggage closed.

I decided to wear the dress I bought in Munich for the cocktail party. I took it out of the tissue and hung it up to shake out any wrinkles. When I went to take my teacup back to the kitchenette, Dad was waking up. He yawned loudly and said he felt he would beg off the cocktail party. He wanted to rest and pack for our flight the next morning. He decided he would order a meal from the nearby restaurant that offered delivery service to the hotel.

Reception called to say that Christian was waiting in the lobby just as I emerged from the bedroom in my new dress. Dad whistled and said Christian would not want me to leave Germany when he saw me in that dress.

Chapter Twenty-Four

CHRISTIAN AND I

THE ELEVATOR OPENED onto a bit of an alcove that hid Reception from view. Christian must have heard the *ding* and the door opening as he turned to greet me. His face lit up as he looked me over and I am sure mine was doing the same. He was wearing a beautiful navy-blue pin-striped suit that fit his tall frame to perfection, with a crisp white shirt set off by a colourful tie.

"Hi," he said as I approached him.

"Hi."

"Ah, the car is just outside. Shall we?" As he reached to open the car door he said, "Oh, should we wait for Rauf?"

I laughed softly. I had forgotten about Dad. "He sends his apologies, but he was tired and wanted to rest and pack for our flight tomorrow morning."

Christian nodded as he went around the car to the driver's side.

It was the first time Christian and I had been alone, and the atmosphere was decidedly different, even a bit awkward. He asked about our day in Hamelin and talked about the time he had taken Julien there when he was ten. The school program of street performers had just started about that time, and it made Hamelin a popular tourist destination. We also talked about the castle and the way of life at that time.

"Germany is a beautiful country, Christian, I'm glad we made this trip."

He smiled. I glanced at his hand on the steering wheel and noticed he was wearing cufflinks. I don't think I've ever dated a man wearing cufflinks, I thought. Was this a date? I was not sure, but whatever it was I knew it would be an interesting evening.

Martin was at the door greeting guests. "Christian, I'm so glad to see you!" He turned and Christian introduced us.

"Welcome, it is a pleasure to meet you. I guess I have you to thank for bringing my friend out tonight! Please enjoy yourselves and I will catch up with you later," he said as he moved to greet other guests.

The restaurant was situated in an old building, but the interior was beautifully appointed while maintaining an old-world charm. We accepted wine from a waiter and moved further into the room. Christian knew several of the guests and introduced me as we wandered around, stopping to chat with people along the way. Eventually, we made our way to a buffet table near the bar. There was a variety of food displayed beautifully, looking delicious. I spotted a chef cooking over a grill and asked what he was making.

"Potato pancakes," he replied. "Oh, I haven't had potato pancakes for years."

He expertly poured the batter on the grill and cooked them to perfection, thin and crisp. He offered sour cream as a topping, and I enthusiastically accepted. Small tables were set up so guests could sit and enjoy their food. A couple motioned that they were finished, and a waiter hurried over to clear their dishes and dust off the linens. We had just settled ourselves at the table when he appeared with more wine. I almost swooned when I bit into the pancakes and Christian chuckled.

"A classy woman with an appetite, I like that." I rolled my eyes and kept eating.

There was an outdoor patio surrounded by trees hung with twinkling lights. A quartet was set up and started playing popular tunes. The music was perfect for the evening and the type of crowd that was there. I was delighted when Christian asked me to dance. We moved smoothly around the dance floor without speaking.

Christian rested his forehead against mine and said, "You look stunning tonight, Sarah."

I smiled. I was glad I had impulsively purchased this dress in Munich, but I did not tell him that. Instead, I said, "As do you."

"I have to say that as beautiful as you look in that dress, you were equally as charming in shorts and a tee shirt the day we went sailing."

This time I laughed aloud and replied, "As did you."

He laughed too and drew me against his chest. Our close physical contact was erotic and sensational. I could feel the last bit of chuckle in his chest and wondered if he felt my heart banging against my ribs. His breathing slowed and I settled comfortably against him. I rested my cheek against his and took in the scent of his aftershave lotion, understated but woodsy, perfect for him. The evening was balmy with a gentle breeze that seemed to move to the music. I closed my eyes and wondered if I was here, in this place at this time with this man holding me in a way that seemed so right. When I opened my eyes the twinkling lights in the trees seemed to wink at me, reassuring me that this was indeed real.

Later the quartet stopped for a break and the crowd started to thin as people prepared to leave. Martin appeared.

"I'm sorry I haven't had a chance to chat with you," he apologized. "Will you join me at the bar for a drink? I'll just say a quick goodbye."

"I don't think I can consume any more alcohol tonight, Christian," I said as we settled on barstools. He agreed and ordered club soda and lime for both of us. Martin joined us a moment later and ordered a martini.

"I have behaved myself all evening, but now it is time to relax," he said with a nod toward the bartender.

"You have a wonderful restaurant, Martin, and the food was delicious," I said as he reached for his drink.

"I'm so glad you enjoyed the evening. You must get Christian to bring you for dinner soon."

"I would love that, but we are returning to Canada tomorrow." At his quizzical look, I told him that my father and I were in Germany on vacation. Christian picked up the narrative and explained that part of the reason for our trip was to examine our ancestral roots in Hamburg.

"As my father is part of a genealogy group he offered to help. That is how we met."

"How is your father, Christian?" He listened as Christian said he was doing quite well.

"I must get around to visiting him one of these days."

He asked me if Joerg had been helpful, and we chatted about ancestors for a few minutes.

"Well," he said sipping his martini, "I sincerely hope that you will return to our fair city someday, Sarah. It would be a pleasure to see you again." Martin made a sideways glance at Christian.

When we got back to the hotel, Christian took my hand to help me out of the car, and he did not release it as we walked into the building. It was incredibly quiet at that hour and the lobby was deserted. In the alcove by the elevator, I turned to him.

"I've had a wonderful time, not just tonight, but throughout our trip. You and your family have been so good to Dad and me. We found more here in Germany than we expected. Thank you, Christian." He put his arm around me.

"I should be thanking you for reminding me that there is life outside of work. I had kind of forgotten that."

A first kiss can be many things— from a gateway to a more intimate relationship to a friendly gesture that both people know will not develop any further. Our first kiss was like a chemical explosion. The second was even more intense if that was possible. But on the third, reality came roaring in like a freight train. I stepped back a pace and placed my hands on his chest, lowering my gaze to his tie. I wanted more, much more, but that was impossible.

"We're leaving in a few hours." A pang of sadness engulfed me. How could such an alluring person come into my life under such strange circumstances only to be snatched away when there was so much more to discover.

He took my hands in his and I raised my gaze to meet his eyes. He kissed my fingers, and I could feel sadness in him as well.

"I hope I'm not being presumptuous, Sarah, but would you consider meeting me in New York in September?"

This could never work; how could this possibly work? I looked into his eyes for a long moment and his expression slowly changed. Of course, this could work! My expression must have changed, too and he smiled and raised his eyebrows slightly.

"Yes, I would consider it." His smile widened and I found myself in his arms. It felt familiar, like an intimate friend, someone I could spend an eternity getting to know. We kissed again, but this time it was more of a goodnight rather than a goodbye.

Chapter Twenty-Five

NOW WHAT?

I WOKE WITH a start and was momentarily disoriented, but the drone of the plane seeped into my senses, and I realized I was on the plane with Dad sitting beside me. He was engrossed in a book but looked up and smiled at me. I had been scrunched in my seat and I sat up trying to ease the kink in my back. I felt gritty and the inside of my mouth felt like I had been chewing cotton. Grabbing my purse from under the seat I said, "I'm going to the lav." Dad smiled and nodded.

I splashed cool water on my face, brushed my teeth, and combed my hair. Feeling better I opened the door to the aroma of freshly brewed coffee, which almost made me salivate. The flight attendant paused to let me pass in front of her before her descent down the aisle. I hurried back to my seat. Dad had tucked his book beside him and already had his tray set up. I put my purse back under the seat and did the same with my tray.

We were served a light meal and taking a sip of coffee, I sat back and exclaimed "Oh, ambrosia!"

Dad laughed. "Late night?"

"Did I wake you when I came in? I tried to be quiet."

"No," but Dad raised an eyebrow at me as he opened his package of plastic utensils.

"The restaurant is Christian's friend's second location in Hamburg and is in a beautiful spot. Last night was the official opening and there were a lot of people there. The food was amazing, and he hired a quartet for dancing. Christian introduced me to several people and the atmosphere was one of celebration. Martin, the owner invited us for a drink as the crowd started to thin and we chatted with him for quite a while. I'm afraid the wine just kept coming and I exceeded my usual consumption."

"It sounds like I would have been a fifth wheel," Dad said examining the food on his tray.

"Is that why you begged off going out last night?"

"Hmm, no, and yes. I was tired, Sarah. It's been a full couple of weeks, but I just thought you and Christian would enjoy a night on your own." He did not say more and neither did I.

After we had eaten, the flight attendant removed our lunch trays and Dad picked up his book after lowering his tray. I retrieved the package Christian gave me with Julien's paper from my carry-on bag in the overhead bin and settled in to read. Julien had written the paper in German, but Christian had gone to the trouble of having it translated while we were in Munich. What a thoughtful man, I mused as I opened the package and got comfortable in my seat. I was engrossed in the story when I noticed Dad's steady breathing beside me. I glanced over to find his book in his lap and him fast asleep. I gently removed his glasses which made him stir a bit, but he was soon asleep again.

I felt warm and content thinking about our time in Germany. It had been a wonderful experience in so many ways, largely due to the Koenig family. I leaned back on the headrest and replayed the previous evening. I had dated a few men since becoming a single woman again, but none that compared to Christian. There had been no one that I felt compelled to continue seeing after a few dates or introducing to my family or friends.

If I dug deep, I had to admit that many of the mistakes in my marriage were mine. I had allowed myself to be dominated by my husband at a cost to my individuality. Whatever personality and character traits my ex-husband has, belong to him, and expecting him to change was just as wrong for him as it had been for me. Dating had not been a priority since my divorce; I was more invested in creating a life for myself and worked hard at achieving that. But there were trust issues, too.

Perhaps it had been the same for Christian after his divorce. He was very committed to the business, but also to his family. I admired that, smiling as I touched the folder in my lap that contained Julien's story. I had known Christian for less than two weeks but had learned a great deal about him in that short time. I frowned thinking about how ridiculous it was to even consider a relationship with him. And yet Christian had invited me to meet him in New York. Could I actually consider doing that? Anyway, it may have been a spur-of-the-moment comment made at the end of a very nice evening. I drifted off to sleep thinking about how those last few moments with him had felt.

We had left Hamburg at ten that morning for a nine-hour fight back to Toronto, but with the time difference, it was only one in the afternoon when we touched down. Dad and I both felt the effects of jet lag. By the time we went through customs, retrieved our luggage, and cabbed into the city, it was late afternoon. The cab dropped Dad off first and it was all I could do to drag my luggage into the house when I finally arrived at my door. The worst part about travelling is, well, travelling.

I noticed a vase with daisies on my dining room table with a note from Ro and Joey welcoming me home. Ro had also stocked my fridge with staples and aired out the house. I dropped my luggage in the den and quickly scanned through the pile of mail Ro had collected and left on my desk.

Laura, from next door, called a bit later to say that Zipper was fast asleep on the window seat in their kitchen, and he was welcome to stay another night while I got settled. She said the girls loved having him there and he seemed quite content, so why disturb him?

I was bone weary, but it was only seven o'clock. I made scrambled eggs and toast, but by eight I was in bed and fast asleep. I slept through until five-thirty on Saturday morning but thought I best get up and back on schedule. I showered and felt human again. I emptied my luggage and separated gifts, started laundry, and put dry cleaning items aside. Dad found room in his luggage for my overflow and called to say he would bring them over on Sunday. I called Ro, Joey was with Tom, and she had a date with Ben that night, but she said she would catch up with me on Sunday, as well.

I was in the den taking a closer look at my mail when Zipper appeared. I laid out food for him and he chowed down but ignored me. He wandered around the house for a bit, but then took his leave, to go back to next door for treats no doubt.

Ro and I were visiting on the front porch on Sunday afternoon when Dad pulled into the driveway. He held out a bag to me and I peeked inside to find my things. He stayed for a bit to visit with Ro but was on his way to Lorna's with the gifts he had gotten for her. I had been telling Ro about our trip and he added his own comments.

"Your dad seems happy, content," said Ro, as Dad backed out of the driveway with a wave and toot of the horn.

I stared into the near distance for a moment.

"It's very interesting, Ro. I mean there will always be the parent/child thing between us, but I've gotten to know Dad in a different way over all this. I love him, of course, but I also like him for the person he is. He will always have that stubborn streak and hold back on his feelings, but he is really a good guy."

Among the things Dad brought over, was a leather handbag I had bought for Ro, along with a soccer tee shirt for Joey. He was involved in soccer, and we found a shirt with the Deutscher Fussball-Bund crest that I knew he would like.

"I'll bring Joey over one night this week, and you can give him the shirt yourself, Sar. He will love it and this bag is gorgeous. Thanks."

"It sounds like this trip was really good for you and your dad, Sarah," she went on. "Even more than you expected."

"A lot of things about it were more than I expected."

I told Ro about meeting the Koenig family; about Christian, Joerg, Hannah, and Julien, and how good they had been to us.

"Hmm, I'm getting the impression there's something you aren't telling me. I'm getting a vibe from you that I don't think I've seen before."

"Do you want to stay for dinner?" I invited. "I have spaghetti in the freezer. Come on in and we can talk while I get it ready."

We sat in the dining room, and I went on about the trip, mostly about Christian. She asked questions here and there but let me go on while she twirled spaghetti.

"Christian is a Caretaker, Ro. He takes care of the people in his life, but with their interests in mind, not to draw attention to him. Several people approached him at the restaurant opening he took me to, and he was gracious, but he did not overdo it. Geez, my ex-husband would have revelled in all that attention and would have forgotten that I was even there, but Christian introduced me to everyone and made sure that I was part of every conversation."

"Sarah, let me understand this. I have never heard you speak about a man like this before. What exactly is going on here? You must see the obvious problem."

"Well, yes, there are a few problems. Dad did not want to mention our relationship with the Meyer family to them. Of course, we did not anticipate spending so much time with the Koenigs, but Dad did not want to get into the part of his history. They are not related to the Meyers, but the families were allies during the time my grandmother lived in their home, and of course, you know what happened there. From the conversations, they just assumed my grandmother emigrated at some point. I am sure they do not know about Eric and the rest of it.

Dad and I did some research on our own, and we did not make much headway, but that does not mean there aren't still some Meyers in Germany who could be related to us. I feel bad that we withheld that information from Christian and his family, but Dad was adamant that he did not want to reveal any of that. I wasn't about to go against Dad's wishes, especially after what happened before and as our relationship is going so well now."

"Ok, I get all that," Ro replied. "But what does it matter? It's not like you're going to see Christian again. Wait, are you?"

"Well, he is doing a crossing to New York in late September on one of his ships and he asked me to meet him there for a weekend."

"Are you seriously thinking of doing that, Sarah? It may just have been something he said at the time."

"I know. It was all I thought about on the trip home, and I was not sure I'd ever hear from him again. But he called yesterday, and we talked for two hours. He mentioned it again and even asked me if I would be comfortable staying on the ship or if I would prefer to be in a hotel."

"Wow, that gives a whole new meaning to the term long-distance relationship. I mean, the man lives in Germany for heaven's sakes. It's not like you'd get to see him very often. What time did he call you yesterday?"

"I don't know. About four o'clock, I think. I was knee-deep in laundry when he called."

"OK, with the time difference it would have been about ten o'clock in Germany. So, he called you on a Saturday night at ten o'clock his time. Hmmm. You said he is divorced?"

"Yes, he's been divorced for about five years. One of the women at the restaurant opening told me they were glad to see him there, as he doesn't usually attend those kinds of things. And Martin, the owner, also seemed surprised to see him with a date. I don't know what to do, Ro. I did not give him a definite answer. Part of me really wants to see him again, but it does seem complicated on so many levels."

"I'll say. I mean his life is in *Germany*." Ro said again. She looked at me closely but didn't say any more. She just grinned.

I was on a roller coaster of emotions during the weeks leading up to the weekend in New York. I went from being glad for the opportunity to see him again to dreading having agreed to it. We got into the habit of talking on Saturdays over the ensuing weeks. Whatever Saturday things I was doing, I always made sure I was home by four o'clock. Ro didn't say much about that, but she seemed to enjoy this new side of me. Her theory was that ten o'clock in Germany was too early to be home from a date and too late to be heading out on a date, especially as we usually talked for a couple of hours. She made a point of determining that this meant he was not seeing anyone.

We had decided that I would spend the weekend on his ship. Christian had given us a tour of the ship he was sailing on, and the staterooms were not large, but well-appointed and comfortable. Koenig Shipping is a generational business, and its predecessors all had their challenges over the decades. I had witnessed first-hand the demise of such businesses in my work at the accounting firm as the generations lost interest in the business or simply thought they would live off the efforts of those who came before them.

Christian did not have the same challenges of the World Wars or the Depression as he took his place in the business, but he was determined to reinvent it as passenger friendly as well as cargo friendly. Cruising was becoming more of a mainstream holiday, where it had once been primarily for the rich and famous, and he wanted to move the business in that direction.

He also endeavoured to make the trip a culinary experience for passengers and Martin had been helpful not only with staff but also with menus. He had numerous thoughts on introducing entertainment and activities, especially for cruises where they were at sea for many days at a time. We talked about these things on our Saturday phone calls. His ambition, commitment, and forward-thinking were things that I found attractive about him, but I was still apprehensive about the weekend. I did not know where in Manhattan my grandmother had spent her first troubled weeks in America with Sophia and her family, but the journals did mention the address where my father was born in New Jersey.

I would have loved to go there just to see what the area was like, this many years later, but I could not discuss this with Christian. I had no choice but to honour Dad's feelings regarding that part of our history.

He asked me a lot of questions about my work and life in Toronto. I talked freely about how much I admire my clients and the satisfaction I feel in helping them with their businesses. He admired my enthusiasm and commitment which made me feel appreciated. We never seemed to run out of things to talk about, and our conversations lasted for hours on those Saturday nights.

I went to the airport directly from the office as my flight left at six pm. It was a short flight to New York, and I arrived by seven thirty. JFK was teeming with people, and I scanned the crowd and felt a bit of panic as I did not see him at first. Then suddenly there he was, and I felt my heart flip over a few times. He embraced me in a hug and kissed my cheek as we elbowed our way through the crowd. I only had hand luggage, so we were able to make our way directly to the exit. He hired a car and I managed to relax a bit as we travelled to the port.

Christian settled me in a stateroom and asked me to meet him in the dining room when I was ready. The passengers had eaten, and most had headed into the city for some nightlife. Dinner was lovely and the chef joined us for coffee afterward. I recognized him from Martin's restaurant and he remembered me from the buffet. Martin sent his regards, which made me feel warm. We talked for hours and then Christian outlined plans for the next day. I was happy to be there and relaxed in Christian's presence, but a bit nervous about what the rest of the evening would entail. Later he escorted me to my stateroom and kissed me goodnight. I stood in the middle of the room not sure if I was relieved or disappointed that he had not ventured in. The other thing I was feeling was exhaustion. It had been a busy week at work and the apprehension I had felt about the weekend caught up with me.

We enjoyed a huge breakfast the next morning and then headed into the city. It was an exciting day with a visit to the top of the Empire State Building, shopping at Bloomingdales, and people-watching at a late lunch in a sidewalk café. Christian had tickets for *Cats* on Broadway for many of the passengers and had saved two for us. We decided to have a late supper after the performance.

I wore a shirt dress in soft camel-coloured wool with a wrap in autumn shades, which was perfect for the theatre. Christian looked as handsome as ever in a dark suit, white shirt, and jaunty tie. We both loved *Cats* and decided it was our favourite live performance of all time. We relaxed over a light meal of crab cakes, salad, and wine in a small bistro. We sat close together across a small table under dim lights and soft music. I was falling fast, and when he took my hand, I felt the same type of energy from him.

He walked me to my stateroom on the ship a few hours later. I fumbled for the key in my handbag, and he took it from me.

"Allow me," he said opening the door. As he put his arm around me, one of the crew came down the corridor.

"Mr. Koenig, Miss," he said in passing. Christian and I looked at each other and laughed.

"Perhaps we should take this inside," he said as we stepped into my room.

"Sarah, I'm glad you agreed to stay on the ship with me this weekend." He hesitated for a moment and then moved closer to me. "Last night—" He searched for words as he touched my arm. "I didn't want you to think that I invited you here just because I wanted to sleep with you."

I moved to set my handbag and wrap on the chair and wiggled out of my shoes.

"I mean, I do want to sleep with you, but only if you feel ready."

I kissed him and removed his suit jacket, laying it over the chair. He took me in his arms. Our phone calls over the past weeks did not offer the sexual tension that people usually feel in the early days of dating when they meet in person. But that's not to say it wasn't there in things we both said, or that it hadn't grown in intensity as the weekend drew closer.

We kissed deeply, desire building. He put his forehead against mine, as he had done on my last night in Hamburg and slowly unbuttoned my dress as I undid his tie. My dress slipped off my shoulders and I moved to the bed to remove my pantyhose. The bed had been turned down and there were chocolates on the pillows.

Christian undressed, leaving on only his shirt, and came to sit beside me. He was wearing cufflinks again and his arm got caught in one of the sleeves as he tried to pull it through.

"Here, let me help with that." I released the cufflink and the shirt ended up on the floor. We stretched out on the bed, and he removed my bra and panties as we explored each other with our mouths, hands, and bodies.

Later, we lay close together, our limbs entwined, completely sated.

"It feels like I'm lying on something," Christian said, rolling onto his back. I laughed as he pulled two chocolates wrapped in gold paper from beneath him. We unwrapped them and popped them into our mouths.

"Yum," I said as I ran my fingers over the soft hair on his chest.

"Indeed" he replied running his hand down the length of my back.

He did not leave my room until ten o'clock on Sunday morning. It had been a long full night, but not nearly long enough. He kissed me and said to meet him in the dining room. I showered and dressed in the comfortable pants and herringbone jacket I had worn for travelling on Friday but switched out the silk blouse for a cream-coloured turtleneck sweater. I packed my things and when I straightened out the bed covers, I noticed something on the floor. I stooped to pick up the cufflink that landed there the night before. It was different from the ones Christian had worn to Martin's party and I turned it in my hand to admire it. The man has good taste, I thought, as I slipped it into my pocket.

He was seated at a table with some guests on the ship. He stood to greet me and held my chair, touching me gently as I took my seat. The couple had been at the theatre the previous night and we chatted about the performance and the trip in general. It was obvious they had enjoyed everything. I watched Christian covertly and could see that he was pleased.

One of the first things I noticed about Christian was his hazel-coloured eyes. Hazel eyes are not common; only about five percent of the population has eyes that colour. He was wearing a multi-coloured light sweater in fall shades of green, brown, gold, and cream, with a deep brown suede bomber jacket that looked as soft as butter. Those colours made his eyes sparkle. The couple said they were going back into the city to do some sightseeing for the afternoon. The ship was sailing at seven that evening for the return trip to Hamburg.

I had to be at the airport by five for my return flight to Toronto. Christian suggested a drive through Central Park before going to the airport. I collected my things from the stateroom and smiled at the fedora I had bought from a street vendor the day before. Not wanting to crush it in my bag I put it on my head and took one last look around, sealing the memory of that room.

The driver found a car park and Christian and I walked leisurely through Central Park among the dog walkers and bikers along a path. We found a bench and sat for a minute.

"Are you tired?" I asked.

"Well, I usually require more than twenty minutes of sleep."

I grinned and remembering his cufflink in my pocket, took it out and handed it to him.

"Oh, where did you find it?" he asked.

"It was on the floor beside the bed."

"Ah, the bed," he smiled. "I'm thinking of having that bed bronzed."

I hadn't blushed since I was a teenager, but I felt my face grow warm. He turned the cufflink in his hand. It was engraved with the letters CK.

"They are different from the ones you wore to Martin's party."

He looked surprised I noticed but didn't say anything.

"I have two pairs. This was my grandfather's, the one that I am named for, and the other pair belonged to my father. They were both from an age of men that dressed in suits everywhere they went."

He looked thoughtful for a moment and then placed the cufflink back in my hand.

"If you keep it, Sarah, you'll have to see me again. You can't expect me to walk around with just one cufflink." He sat back and put his arm along the back of the bench, then faced me. I looked at the cufflink and smiled, but then a frown took its place.

"We will just have to figure it out as we go along," he said. "Will you consider it?"

I closed my hand around the cufflink. "Yes, I will consider it."

Chapter Twenty-Six

NEAR, FAR WHEREVER YOU ARE

THE NEXT YEAR was the best, the absolute best. Christian and I saw each other as often as possible. At times we laughed and played like children and at others, we were serious and multi-layered. Our physical connection never wavered, whether we lay wrapped together, the feel of our skin warm and damp, or if we caught a glimpse of each other from a distance. At times we chattered like magpies and at others, we enjoyed comfortable silence. If we travelled by car or rail, Christian would take my hand in his as we sat next to each other as the miles passed by. He fell asleep beside me on a train, and I watched the steady rise and fall of his chest while his dark lashes lay against his face.

We spent our first Christmas in Toronto, where I introduced him to the rest of my family and friends.

Then off to Montreal to spend New Year's Eve with Mike and Marc. Marc's restaurant was hosting a party and the evening was full of laughter, noise, and music with delicious food at the ready all evening. Balloons, glitter, and streamers cascaded from the ceiling. Our kiss at midnight started the New Year off with the promise of more to come. The air was fresh, the streets full of people in party mode, as we walked to our hotel a few blocks away. We were on a high after all the excitement of the evening and burned off our energy in the best possible way.

Sleeping in late on New Year's Day, we decided to order room service. Showered and wrapped in white fluffy hotel robes, we sat at a table by the window looking out at a world of sunshine that reflected and sparkled on frost and snow. How natural we seem together, I thought, as I admired him, his hair still wet from the shower.

As if reading my thoughts he said, "I love the way you look in the morning."

Our flights were booked for approximately the same time later that day, but our gates were at opposite ends of the departure area. We set our bags down and faced each other. The airport was busy with people hurrying around us dragging luggage and looking at their watches, but it felt like we were alone. Christian took me in his arms for a long hug.

"You are a talented hugger," I said smiling into his eyes. He looked at me for a long moment.

"This has been an amazing week." He hesitated for a heartbeat. "This isn't the place and not what I planned, but I can't leave without telling you how I feel." A pause, then he continued, "I closed myself off, didn't really want to get involved with anyone, concentrated on work. But there is something about you, I think I realized it the day we went sailing." He took a breath, "I love you."

We kissed long and deep and then again.

"I didn't expect this either, but I love you, too."

We met in airports, and I never failed to hold my breath waiting in the crowd to meet him or stepping off a plane into a sea of faces. There was always a moment of panic, what if something happened and he wasn't there? I remember feeling rooted to the spot in an airport somewhere, I couldn't breathe, couldn't move until he appeared. His handsome face lit up when he saw me. My breath escaped in a long sigh as he hugged me, and a tear ran down my face. He captured the tear on his thumb and kissed my cheek where it had landed.

We travelled to Florida, spent a few days with Dad and Lorna, rented a car, and explored the state all the way to Key West. We had so much fun in that quirky, campy town, and vowed to bring Hannah there. It was picture-perfect for her.

That summer I spent a month in Hamburg. Christian and I went to Switzerland and Italy by rail but made Hamburg our home base. We would have coffee together in the morning and Christian would leave for his office. The time difference meant that I had to wait until later in the day to contact my office. I would take long walks on those mornings and made friends with Hamburg on my own. One day I found myself at the Koenig Inn. I put my hands on the rod iron fence and was transported back to the time my grandmother lived here. It was almost as though I could remember those days. Tears blurred my vision as I thought about the turmoil, she had endured in the last years she was there, but it was overshadowed somehow by the fact that I felt she was happy I was here.

Joerg was not an early riser, but by the time I returned to the house, Marta had arrived and would prepare a brunch for the two of us. I enjoyed those times with Joerg. His health was failing, but his mind was as sharp as ever. On that particular morning, I may have been a bit pensive after visiting the Koenig Inn and he looked at me carefully, placing his gnarled hand on mine. He appeared to enjoy spending time with me as much as I did with him.

Christian offered his home office, and I would retire there in the early afternoon to touch base with my office and deal with whatever was going on with staff and clients. Later Christian would settle Joerg for the evening and he and I would go out for dinner. We went to Martin's restaurant, and he welcomed me with a big hug, lifting me off my feet. He felt like an old and dear friend.

Later that month, we flew to Munich with Julien. He wasn't starting university until the following year, but Christian had arranged to meet with an advisor to discuss his program and make sure Julien was taking the appropriate courses to prepare for university. He wanted Julien to live in residence his first year, so we toured the campus and found the dorm rooms adequate. The university was old and beautiful, and all three of us were impressed by its presence. Julien could not stop talking about it and his enthusiasm was infectious.

We spent time with Hannah, went sailing again on the North Sea, and took a short cruise to England on one of Christian's ships. I returned to Toronto with a deeper feeling of attachment not only to Christian but to his family and city as well.

Christian did another crossing to New York and arranged the same stateroom for me where we spent our first night together. It felt ethereal when I walked in, and I shivered a bit. There was a package on the nightstand.

"I got you something."

Sitting on the bed I frowned but opened the package where I found a small bronze bed with two chocolates wrapped in gold. I burst out laughing knowing this article would become one of my most precious belongings. Still laughing I reached into my bag and handed him a parcel.

"I brought you something, too." Smiling, he opened it and lifted out the gold cufflink.

"I hope you don't mind, but I had it engraved on the back. It belonged to your grandfather, who was connected to my grandmother."

He turned it over and saw the word 'connected' in a small script.

"Yes, connected," he said with a smile.

As connected to Christian as I felt I had never discussed my grandmother's complete story with him. I wanted to and being in New York again would have been the ideal time, but I was torn between honouring my father's wishes and being transparent with Christian. It may me feel uneasy, but the moment passed.

When we were not able to be together, we would stay connected by phone. Christian had an international phone line that he linked to his home office. He set up a corporation he called the Koenig Group, which incorporated Hannah's ever-expanding business as well as the Koenig Inn. She would call me with questions on how to handle certain aspects of the business. She wanted to start manufacturing her furniture and fixture designs herself and called Dad for advice on that part of things.

Christian apologized, saying she had advisors, but Dad and I didn't mind. We were both interested in what her next scheme would be. The people in his world became part of mine and vice versa. Sometimes Dad would chat with Joerg. They had not finished their chess game from our first visit to Hamburg and had continued it by mail, which we all thought was bizarre, but Christian said Joerg looked forward to the mail to see what Dad's next move would be. They would question each other's moves on phone chats.

Ro and Ben got married in the spring. Christian came for the wedding and brought Hannah and Julien with him. Joerg was not up to the trip. The wedding was splendid; Joey walked Ro down the aisle dressed in a suit and wearing a huge grin.

Ro looked beautiful in an understated dress that suited her perfectly and she had flowers in her curls. I was Maid of Honour and cried as they took their vows. The reception was so much fun. We all ate, drank, and danced for hours. Julien, at seventeen, was a hit with the ladies, and they all wanted to dance with him. He had outgrown some of his shyness and there were definite signs of the man he would become in his composure and attitude. He was excited about starting university in Munich that fall. Hannah was also a hit with her sense of style and excess.

Ro, Ben, and Joey went to Alaska that summer. Ben was supervising a job in Fairbanks, but they carved out time to tour the interior, going to Denali, Mt. McKinley, and out to the coast to go whale watching in Juneau, viewing the totem poles in Ketchikan, and visit the gold mining town of Skagway.

Christian, Hannah, Julien, and I toured Toronto Island, the CN Tower, and other highlights in Toronto after the wedding. We rode the Maid of the Mist at Niagara Falls and spent a night in Niagara on the Lake. Christian had described Mike's artwork to Hannah from our New Year's visit to Montreal and she noticed the abstract hanging in my house in the Beaches. In Hannah-like fashion, she carried on about insisting that she meet Mike. Christian changed her return ticket to Hamburg and got a flight from Toronto to Montreal and return to Hamburg from there.

I called Mike and Marc and warned them of her visit, but the three of them hit it off right away. Hannah loved Mike's use of colour and how he combined different hues to almost create new colours. She literally took a painting off the wall in their loft and two more from the restaurant and had them shipped to Germany.

Mike called me very excited, as Hannah had also commissioned him to do some designs for wallpaper that she might want to add to her line. I was thrilled that they had gotten on so well and couldn't help but be pleased with yet another connection in our families.

Chapter Twenty-Seven

NOW YOU KNOW THE REST OF THE STORY

JOERG DIED LATE in November of that year. The news hit us hard. Joerg's health had been declining even more, and when he suddenly developed pneumonia, Christian rushed him to the hospital. Julien wanted to return to Hamburg, but he was finishing his first semester and had exams to prepare for. Christian assured him that Joerg was where he needed to be and was comfortable. He responded well at first but took a sudden turn for the worst and died quietly.

I was in the middle of a difficult and complicated matter at work. One of our long-term corporate clients was getting a divorce, and we were required to do a Business Valuation as part of the divorce proceedings. We had several meetings with him and his lawyers, where he barked and howled at every turn. He, a man in his sixties, decided that he wanted to marry a woman the same age as his eldest son. Everyone was stressed; it was all the office talked about for weeks and my boss was heard muttering, "there's no fool, like an old fool," as we laboured through the process.

Just as we thought everything was sorted out, his wife decided she wanted trust funds set up for the grand-children before she would agree to the divorce. We had a horrible meeting with everyone's lawyers, the client and his wife, and our team. The lawyers were yelling, and our client was red-faced and pacing, while we were trying to keep the whole thing from imploding. The wife was the calmest one in the room.

We had an impartial position in the divorce, but I couldn't help but admire the wife. Her demeanour was quiet, but she proved to be a fierce Momma Bear whose sole purpose was to protect her family. She was not pre-pared to go quietly into the night until she knew they would be looked after. I think my boss felt the same way as we struggled to keep everyone happy. Numbers don't lie, and this divorce was going to cost him plenty. My boss was overheard telling him that he hoped it was worth it.

I pleaded with my boss for some time off to attend Joerg's funeral, not only for Christian's sake but mine, as well, as I had grown very fond of Joerg. He was not happy about it. Everyone wanted this mess to be cleaned up by the end of the year, but he agreed to no more than a few days when I promised to take part of the file with me to work on during the flights.

Christian was also stressed. Julien was grief-stricken that he had not been there at the end, and Christian felt it was his fault for assuring Julien that Joerg was managing. Christian wanted to fly to Munich to bring Julien home, but Julien insisted he would fly on his own, while Christian made the necessary arrangements in Hamburg. Julien had not flown by himself before, but it was a short commuter flight and Christian finally agreed.

Dad was also heartbroken and called me back an hour after he got the news to say he wanted to go with me to Hamburg. At the last minute, Lorna said she wanted to go, too. She had not met Joerg but was fond of Christian, and supportive of both Dad and me.

We scrambled for flights and were leaving the following morning. I got a seat separate from them so I could spend my time in the air concentrating on the file. Christian met us at the airport. Dad and Lorna had booked a room in the same hotel we had stayed in on our first trip to Hamburg and they left to check-in. Julien's flight was due an hour later, so Christian and I waited to greet him when he touched down. Christian was distraught and paced anxiously waiting for Julien's arrival. I had not seen Julien since the spring and the tall handsome young man that stepped off the flight took my breath away. He was obviously thriving at university, but the boy in him showed through as he and Christian embraced and shed a few tears. He hugged me and said how glad he was that I had come.

The funeral was well attended and solemn. Joerg was well known in Hamburg and many people came to pay their final respects. There was a reception after the service. Julien had to catch a return flight to Munich, so Christian and I took him to the airport. We were meeting Hannah, Dad, and Lorna at the Koenig Inn later for dinner.

Everyone was subdued over dinner. Lorna was intrigued by the Inn and asked a few questions about it. She had her own vision of the Inn from my grandmother's journals and my description but was fascinated to see it in person. Hannah quietly discussed the renovations, while the rest of us tried to enjoy the meal. After dinner, we returned to the house in Altstadt and settled in the living room. Marta had attended the funeral but had not approached Christian. She was at the house. After she made coffee, she took Christian aside and offered her condolences, tearfully telling him how much she had enjoyed tending to Mr. Joerg and how much he would be missed. Christian said he would no longer need her services but gave her a large bonus and offered recommendations to any future employers on her behalf. He asked me to fetch brandy from the study, while he excused himself to call Julien to make sure he arrived safely in Munich.

Dad offered to help, but we stood in the study for a few minutes before opening the liquor cabinet, glancing at Joerg's favourite chair and the chess set sitting on the side table.

"Another soul lost to us," Dad said barely above a whisper. We stood for another moment, each lost in our own thoughts. I glanced at Joerg's beloved garden through the French doors, but it looked as forlorn at this time of year as our thoughts.

Christian joined us in the living room.

"Julien is fine, still a bit shaken by all this, but he has a busy schedule so that should keep him distracted. We'll talk again tomorrow." He was carrying a large brown envelope. "Rauf, I found this among my father's things. I think he meant for me to mail it to you, but since you are here, I'll give it to you now."

"What is it?" Dad asked as Christian passed it to him.

"I don't know, I never saw it before yesterday when I was looking for something on his desk, but it is addressed to you." Dad turned it over and broke the seal on the back. He took out an 8 x 10 black and white photo with a note clipped to it, with a message that read, "I thought this might be of interest to you. All the Best, Joerg."

Dad studied the photo for a moment and turned visibly pale and shaken.

"Dad?" He passed it to me, and I knew immediately who it was. Reinhold Meyer was centred in the photo with a younger man on each side. To his left, a serious-looking young man in an army uniform, on his right a dapper younger man in a suit and straw hat of those times with a cheeky grin. I turned it over and read Reinhold, Hans, and Rauf Meyer—1913. I silently passed it to Lorna.

Christian and Hannah were both puzzled by our reaction. Lorna looked at Dad but passed the photo to Christian. He and Hannah both looked at it, but it didn't seem to mean anything to them.

"My father was quite nostalgic in his last weeks," said Christian. "He talked a lot about the past, which I think is not uncommon when someone is reaching the end of their life. He also looked at a lot of old documents and photos. But I wonder why he wanted you to have this particular photo?"

In the meantime, Hannah was studying both the photo and Dad intently.

"There seems to be an uncanny resemblance between you and the men in this photo, especially the younger man." She turned it over and said, "The one named Rauf."

Dad sighed and stood to pace the room. He looked at Lorna and me, bowed his head, and started to speak in a hesitant voice. His sentences ran into each other as he paced and told the story of our relationship with the Meyer family. He jumped back and forth in the telling and paused to gather his thoughts in places. Christian and Hannah glanced back and forth at each other, Lorna, and me, but did not interrupt.

When Dad paused to finish his brandy, Hannah said, "I vaguely remember my grandmother, Julia talking about them to my mother one time. Julia was a young girl in 1913 but she would have known the Meyer family. If I remember correctly, she said something about Reinhold Meyer having lost both his sons, one to the war and the other who disappeared, and no one ever heard from him again. She said Reinhold died a broken and unhappy man."

Christian refilled everyone's brandy glasses and Dad continued the story, explaining the birth of Erik, my grandmother being expelled from the Koenig home, her voyage to America leaving Erik behind, and her reunion with Rauf. He disclosed that he did not know that he was Rauf's son or that Rauf died in the years of the Spanish flu in New Jersey until recently. By the time he got to my grandmother's marriage to William and their emigration to Canada, he was exhausted and fell back into his chair.

It felt like the oxygen had been pulled out of the room and everyone was waiting to exhale.

Dad and Lorna had plans to stay on for another week and had train tickets to travel south to the Black Forest area the following morning.

"I think we've all had a very stressful few days," said Lorna. "Perhaps we should leave."

As they rose, Dad picked up the photo, put it back in the envelope, and tucked it under his arm.

"I'm very sorry for your loss, Christian, and that all of this has come up at such an inappropriate time. Your father will be missed."

Hannah rose as well and said she would drive them to the hotel.

I was about to speak, but Christian stopped me and said we should get some rest. Neither of us slept well, though. I could not shut my mind down but must have dozed off at some point. When I awoke Christian wasn't there. I found him in the study sitting in Joerg's favourite chair with a coffee and the newspaper. I poured a coffee for myself and sat across from him. There was a cold rain falling outside the French doors. It felt as dismal as the atmosphere in the study. Christian folded his newspaper and set it aside, then looked up allowing me to speak.

"There is more to the story, Christian," I said. I told him everything starting with the box and journals and the odd way in which it had come into my hands. Dad had not referred to my duplicity in withholding this information from him and the rift it had caused between us, but I filled him in on that. "He was so mad, so hurt. He didn't talk to me for months. My brother Dave didn't want to get involved. He was content to leave the past in the past, but Mike stood by me."

"Why did you come here, Sarah?"

"I wanted to come. My grandmother died when I was a young girl, and I had a great deal of difficulty reconciling her earlier life with the woman I knew. I wanted to walk where she walked and see for myself the world in which she grew up. I convinced Dad to come with me; he was aware of some of her story, but not all. I thought it would be a way for him to heal, but also for the two of us to reconnect. It was Lorna who convinced Dad to talk to me about it."

"What does Lorna have to do with all this?"

"Lorna is Katie's mother, you met Katie and Ian in Toronto. She's a retired teacher, born here in Germany and she is bilingual. My grandmother's journals were written in German, and I couldn't read them. Ro introduced me to Lorna. She was volunteering at Katie and Ro's school in the Beaches and Ro thought she would help me."

He ran his hands through his hair and stood.

"Lorna translated the journals for me. We were only part way through them when my mother died. I told you she died in Florida, and everything was such a shock—such a mess. I couldn't tell Dad about it then, he was too upset, but I had to see it through. It was months later when I finally told Dad about the journals. He didn't know he had a brother that my grandmother had to leave behind when she fled to New Jersey to find Rauf."

Christian paced the study, his expression dark and confused.

"Dad left for Florida for another winter without things being resolved between us. Lorna was in Florida at the same time and looked him up. You see, she felt bad for the role she played in helping me and confronted Dad about it. I went to Florida and the three of us hashed it all out. Dad was still upset, but if it hadn't been for Lorna, I'm not sure it ever would have been resolved."

He was getting more agitated by the minute. We had disagreed about things from time to time, but nothing like this.

"But why did you come to my family? Was it to see for yourself what kind of people would throw a young girl with a child out in the cold with no resources?" Christian's expression was dark, and he raised his voice. I had never seen him like this.

Tears were pouring down my face.

"On the contrary, Christian. Her writings described how happy she had been working and living with your family. Your great-grandmother Anna protected her as long as she could. I'm sure that Anna hoped that if Reinhold Meyer knew that she had given birth to his grandson, it may have helped him to reunite with his son Rauf. It was Meyer who insisted that my grandmother be removed from the house, not your great-grandfather Albert. I'm not even sure if Albert was aware that she had a child and that Erik lived in the house."

"Not knowing what goes on in the Koenig household seems to be an epidemic," Christian said with anger in his voice.

"When we discovered that your family was still in the shipping business—then Joerg's name showed up as part of the genealogy group here in Hamburg, we thought we could meet with him and perhaps he could give us direction in doing more research. The generosity and kindness your family has shown us has gone a long way in helping Dad come to terms with his past. In fact, he decided while we were here on that first trip to forgo any further efforts in pursuing the Meyer history. He feels no connection to them."

"God, Sarah, all these people know about this. What must they think of us?"

"Katie doesn't know the whole story," I said lamely. "Christian, I had no idea that coming here would lead me to you. We love your family, they have come to mean a great deal to us, to me. I love you with all of my heart." I started to cry again.

"I would like to believe that Sarah." When he saw how stricken I was by that remark he said, "I do believe that is true, but I also feel that you don't trust me. Obviously, your father resolved his feelings, reconciled with you, and even developed a relationship with Lorna. Don't you think I would have helped you in whatever way I could? You mentioned you knew where your father was born in New Jersey. We were in New York, twice. We could have gone to New Jersey to see what we could find."

There was definite anger in his voice and his demeanour, and it was making me angry, too.

"I wanted to, Christian, but it is Dad's story, and up to him to reveal it when he was ready."

Christian turned his back to me and stared out the French doors.

"No, it's your story, Sarah, and you didn't feel you could share it with me," he said in a low quiet voice that scared me more than when he had been shouting.

I felt defeated, angry, and exhausted. I looked at the clock.

"My flight leaves in a few hours. I left Toronto in a hurry, and I have an important meeting tomorrow that I still have to prepare for."

"I'll take you to the airport," he said.

He walked me into the terminal and set my luggage down at the security gate.

"I am truly sorry for all this and your loss. Joerg was a wonderful man, and he will be missed."

"Goodbye, Sarah. Have a safe trip home." He kissed me but there wasn't much energy behind it.

The following weeks were busy, both at work cleaning up that messy file, and with events leading up to Christmas. Dad and I were going to Mississauga on Christmas Day, and he was leaving a few days later for Florida. Lorna was going with him to spend the winter. She was also busy getting ready for Christmas with Katie and Ian but showed up at my door unexpectedly one afternoon.

"Sarah, you look pale. You've been holed up since you came back from Germany. Come for a walk with me."

We chatted about the week she and Dad had spent in Germany after Joerg's funeral. They spent most of it in Frankfurt where they picked up gifts at a Weihnachtsmarkt and then toured the city. They did manage a side trip to Seligenstadt where Lorna was born, but it had been a cold rainy day so they couldn't do much exploring.

"We called Christian before we left Germany," said Lorna.

"I know, Dad told me. But he said Christian was quiet and introspective."

"Have you heard from him?"

"Yes, he called the day after I got home but we didn't talk for long. And I haven't heard from him since."

"Give him time," said Lorna. "He'll come around. Men can be stubborn and set in their ways, especially German men."

I laughed. "Tell me about it. I was raised by one that we all know quite well."

"But they are very loyal once they get over themselves," Lorna said with a grin.

"Obviously Joerg made a connection between my father and the picture in the envelope. I wonder why he didn't share that with Christian," I mused.

"I have a theory," Lorna said. "You said that Joerg's physical health had not been good for some time, but there was nothing wrong with his mind, right?"

I nodded. "Absolutely. Anyone who could play chess by mail is sharp. He also wrote letters to me and whenever we spoke on the phone, he was very coherent."

"Well, when Hannah saw that picture the day of his funeral, it triggered a memory from when she was a young girl. Joerg was a generation closer to your grandmother's time. He may have remembered something. Sarah, you said that Christian told you when Hannah's parents died, whatever family memorabilia such as pictures and documents they had, came into Joerg's hands. He may have remembered seeing that picture."

"Christian also said Joerg spent his last weeks looking through old pictures and documents," I added.

"Joerg may have suspected the Meyer connection for some time but wanted that picture for confirmation. I mean it wasn't a big stretch with the resemblance being so strong and them having the same name. He may have wanted to give your father the opportunity to speak of the matter himself, which is why he did not discuss it with Christian. He intended to mail it to your father and let him decide. Christian would not have thought anything of it, as he mailed things for him all the time. What did his note say, Sarah, I can't remember?"

"Something to the effect that Dad may find the picture interesting, and he wished him all the best."

"Pretty cryptic, but Joerg may have felt it was time to come clean as you and Christian have been seeing each other for some time." Lorna touched my arm with affection. "Sarah, relationships come in all shapes and sizes, and at different times in life. Like this thing with your father and I."

I looked closely at her.

"We just drifted together, it surprised both of us. You know I would never try to replace your mother, Sarah."

I stopped dead in my tracks.

"Lorna, I've never thought that. You are so good for Dad and I love you to pieces. You have become a very special person to me, one in a million."

I took her arm and leaned against her.

"Your father is a good man, and he is good for me, too. Men like him come with a hard outer shell, they were raised that way, but he loves you and your brothers very much. He was devastated over the rift with you, and frankly, with Mike confirming that he is gay. He simply didn't know how to handle it. It broke his heart that he treated both of you the way he did and blamed himself.

I think Christian is a lot like him, which may be why you love him. You told me he is the caretaker, but you didn't give him the chance to take care of you. We all need to be taken care of from time to time. You are a strong woman, my darling, and independent, but don't rob him the opportunity to love you in that way."

Tears spilled over my face, and I had a giant lump in my throat.

"Lorna, how did you get so wise?"

"I'm not that wise, just experienced, and I love you so very much. I just want to see you happy."

I kissed her cheek and we laughed as we continued arm in arm along the lake in the cold frosty air.

"I'm not trying to tell you what to do, Sarah, far from it," Ro said over dinner a few days later.

"What do you mean?" I asked.

"This long-distance thing with you and Christian," Ro continued. "I mean, where is it leading, Sarah? The time you spend together is usually in holiday mode. That isn't real life. You haven't experienced a day-to-day relationship. Everyone has disagreements, which is actually how couples get to know each other, but you and

Christian haven't experienced that. Have you discussed your future in any depth?" she continued.

"You've known each other long enough that most couples would consider enough time to make decisions about what you want out of the relationship. This whole thing is the first real conflict you and Christian have had but being so far away from each other makes it impossible to sit down in person and hash it out. Ben and I don't always agree, and we're still getting used to being married. It takes work, Sarah. Ben and I both lived very independent lives and I brought a child into the marriage. It's not easy, but it's worth the effort. Anything worth having takes commitment and has to be nurtured."

I sighed. "I know Ro, but I guess I'm just confused."

"My money is on you, girlfriend. You'll figure it out." She winked at me.

Christmas came and went, and I found myself at home alone one evening. My friends were making plans for New Year's Eve, but I couldn't get into the spirit of it. Mike invited me to Montreal, but I wasn't in the mood for a boisterous evening as it would only remind me of the time Christian and I had spent New Year's Eve at Marc's restaurant.

I hadn't made much of an effort to decorate the house for Christmas, and it looked as grumpy as I felt. I put a log in the fireplace, lit a bayberry candle, and poured a glass of wine. Zipper was stretched out on the sofa, his front and back legs making his body seem very long. He was fast asleep and snoring softly.

I settled in the chair with my legs tucked under me, covered with the Afghan from the back of the sofa.

I sipped my wine and stared into the burning log as it crackled in the fireplace and thought about Christian. I went to my bedroom and got the bronze bed that I kept on my dresser. I looked at it on my palm and thought about the first night we spent together and all the time since then. I doubted that I would ever love another man the way I loved him, a love that was now very fragile.

I also loved his family. Joerg had been a good friend and I smiled at the memory of our quiet talks. I would miss him and remember him with nostalgia. I was crazy about Julien and really wanted to experience his journey into manhood. And of course, there was Hannah, a woman like no other with her ambition, talent, and electric personality. You can tell a lot about a person by the people who love them, and Christian was well loved by these people. The void that all of these people would leave was incomprehensible.

I had earned my independence and knew I could take care of myself, but it wasn't enough anymore. I thought about what Lorna said. The thought of being cared for by Christian and caring for him was not at all unpleasant.

Another thought had been simmering in the back of my mind that I had tried to tramp down but could no longer ignore. Lorna also said that time goes by quickly. I had been with the accounting firm for more than fifteen years and had been thrilled when I was promoted to Senior Manager. But if I was honest with myself, I didn't enjoy the work as much as I had in the early days. I no longer met with clients and in fact, I didn't even know some of the newer ones beyond their balance sheets and financial statements.

I missed the days when I had gone with a briefcase in hand to meet these hard-working entrepreneurs in their environment. My recent experience with the corporate client and his divorce had left me drained and saddened. I had not shared this feeling with anyone and was only beginning to come to terms with it myself.

I poured another glass of wine. Ro was also right. Anything worth having required work. Was I prepared to put in the work? Was Christian? He said I didn't trust him, and perhaps he felt I didn't need him. This couldn't be the end. I wanted to move on with my life, but the future felt empty, dull. I may be my father's daughter and inherited his stubbornness, but I also have my grandmother's blood flowing through my veins. She never gave up and I wouldn't either.

It was late; the log had burned down in the fireplace. My second glass of wine was empty, and I was very close to crying, when the phone rang, startling both Zipper and me.

"Sarah, did I wake you? I really need to talk to you."

Chapter Twenty-Eight

MOVING ON

I DID SUCCUMB to a crying jag the night Christian called, and he was upset too. Our conversation was a bit stilted at first, but the flood gates opened, and we talked for hours that night and the days following. In February, we met in the Caribbean on the island of St. Lucia for a ten-day holiday. He arrived the night before, and when I stepped off the transfer van from the airport, he was there waiting for me. I wasn't nervous and didn't panic. I went into his arms with the knowledge that this was the most real thing in my world. We had a bungalow in a resort on the north end of the island with wide doors that we could open to capture a view of the water and breezes. Our patio was alive with bougainvillea and greenery.

It was an idyllic time; we went snorkelling, swimming, and sailing, walked the beach, and went to the market in Castries where I bought sundresses and had my hair plaited with beads like the natives. Christian showed his silly side by buying brightly printed shirts, which I insisted looked good on him. We enjoyed nightly dinners and entertainment under a sky filled with stars and warm breezes filled with the aroma of the island. We talked for hours at a time and fell asleep in deep contentment.

Christian talked about his marriage to Julien's mother, Angela. When Julien was in school full time, she took an interest in charities. He supported the charities that she favoured, and still does, but did not enjoy the fundraising and gala events as much as she did. She was in her element, but Christian felt these events were excuses for people to get dressed up and hobnob with the 'who's who' in Hamburg.

The charities benefited from the galas, but Christian found some of the people dull and tiring. If he was at sea when an event like that came up, Angela would go on her own, and eventually, she found her second husband at one of those events. He is a lawyer, much older than her, with political ambitions. So now she travels all over the country with him enjoying life in the limelight.

"Eventually the fundamental differences in our personalities led to other things," he said. "She's happy in that life and it hasn't changed the one thing we did agree on, which is Julien. They spend time in Munich and make a point of seeing him as often as possible."

"Does Julien like her new husband?" I asked.

"He gets along with him, but Julien thinks he's a bit of a stuffed shirt with a practiced smile." Christian laughed. "At least that's the impression I get. Julien has no interest in politics, so they don't have a lot in common."

"Do you think Julien will come into the family business?" I asked.

"I hope so, Sarah, but I want him to find his own way. I think he'd like to work in the electronics field for a while after he graduates to gain some experience. Every generation has faced different challenges in the shipping business with changing times. My father wasn't too happy when I wanted to add passenger travel. It cost a lot of money to refit the ships and we've done it slowly to see how profitable it is."

"I think you did the right thing by concentrating on the common areas and dining room. I think passengers want to spend most of their time in areas where they can mingle with other guests and enjoy the amenities."

"That's exactly the way I see it, but it took time for my father to accept the concept. I think Julien will want to revolutionize the industry electronically, and I'm afraid I won't understand it." He laughed. "We will probably have the same issues I had with my father."

I told him about my marriage to Ron.

"We got married too quickly; we hardly knew each other, and it turned out that we are different in many ways. He's a lot of flash, where I'm more function, I guess. I told him about the 'ice palace' and how he tried to manipulate me in my work.

"I wanted to make my own decisions, but he wasn't willing or able to support me in that way."

He laughed softly. "You've done very well for yourself in your profession. You should be proud of your accomplishments. I'm sure it wasn't easy. I think your clients appreciate what you've done for them and the way you approach things. Hannah certainly does, and she isn't the easiest person to work with." He laughed again and looked thoughtful.

I hesitated for a long moment and he waited for me to speak.

"There is something I have not discussed with anyone, Christian."

He waited patiently for me to find the right words.

"I was thrilled when I was promoted to Senior Manager with the firm. That is a huge stepping-stone in the accounting world, and I did work hard to get there."

"But…," he said when I failed to elaborate.

"But recently I've had feelings of discontent. I miss the client contact. I spend most of my time supervising a staff, which I do enjoy, but it's not the same—not as much fun as the days when I knew my clients and worked closely with them. I have not verbalized these feelings, Christian; I'm not sure where I'm going with this.

I'm quite certain my colleagues would not understand, and my family and friends would probably think I'm crazy to feel like this. Accountants, by their very nature, tend to be introverts who enjoy the work but are not always good with people. But I felt part of the creative process when I worked closely with clients, enjoyed their successes, and got a lot of satisfaction in the role I played in their achievements. It was an ongoing thing with a lot of clients as their businesses evolved and we worked together to find ways to make that happen."

"Perhaps you've got what you needed out of that, and it's time to move on. Have you thought of opening your own business?" asked Christian.

"Yes, I've even done a business plan, but I would need a number of clients to make it viable and I may end up in the same place at the end of the day, managing the business rather than being an active part of it."

"That's interesting. I've met women in positions of power in business, as you are, over the years and it can make them hard, even hostile. I don't see you like that."

"Women are coming into their own more and more, Christian, rather than being an appendage to men, which makes life interesting, but it can be tough. The only power I want is the power to be myself; I want to work and achieve success, certainly, but to have fun doing it. I want to be more hands-on and enjoy the ride."

I looked at him and smiled, breaking the sombre mood.

"It feels good to talk about this, instead of living inside my own head."

We both laughed and the subject turned to other things.

The resort offered a shuttle to a sister resort which they had on the northernmost tip of the island, and a few days later we decided to see what that resort had to offer. We took a long swim and settled on lounges under a tiki roof out of the sun. A waiter came along with a tray of exotic drinks which we accepted.

"This looks more like a fruit salad than a drink," said Christian, looking at the pile of fruit with a tiny umbrella on the top.

"If you like your fruit salad laced with rum," I said, taking a sip.

We settled back on the lounges and watched as a speed boat raced by with a water skier expertly jumping the waves in its wake.

"Sarah, would you allow me to read your grandmother's journals?" he asked, setting his drink on the table.

I looked at him in surprise. "Is that something you would like to do?"

"I've been thinking about her a lot. I would like to read them. With your father's permission, too, of course."

"Some people may think that what she did was wrong, but I admire her courage and tenacity. She came from a simple life but dared to take such a tremendous leap of faith. Such bravery in a woman, a young woman at that, was ground-breaking for those times. Even her marriage to William was such a brave thing to do, but she did it to protect herself and my dad." I sighed. "She did what she could for Erik, too, and the rest of her family to the best of her ability. I wish I had been older and knew her better before she died, and that she had told us about Erik."

"Those were very different times, and even though both you and your father have told the story, I would really like to read it in her words. I'm only sorry that my father isn't here to share that with me."

"Yes, I think Joerg would have enjoyed it. Such an intelligent and insightful man. I would like for you to read it, Christian, and I'm sure Dad would as well. I'll ask him when I get home."

"I would prefer to ask him myself. If it is all right with you, I'll call him."

Our time on St. Lucia was coming to an end. We were having breakfast on the patio on one of our last days there. There were a few errant clouds that we knew would be gone in an hour, leaving a flawless blue sky, turning cerulean as it met the water on the horizon. The sun sparkled on the water and there was a lone sailboat wandering calmly and aimlessly on its voyage to nowhere in particular.

I felt Christian's gaze and turned to find him looking pensive. He set his coffee cup down on the table.

"Sarah, I never properly apologized to you for my behaviour after my father died. I hurt you which is something I never want to do."

"It was such a difficult time for all of us, and I am just as much to blame. You were right, it is my story. The timing certainly didn't help matters, losing Joerg as we did."

"I was upset with him for not sharing his suspicions with me about your relationship to the Meyer family, but I realize he probably wanted to allow your dad to decide how to handle it. Your dad was put in an awkward spot, and my reaction didn't help matters." He flashed a grin and said, "Perhaps it helped you and I develop a better way of dealing with disagreements."

"We certainly know how to make up!" I said as we both grinned. "But I don't ever want to feel that way again. I hurt you, too, by not trusting you. You didn't deserve that. Let's not ever do that again."

"I want more," he said.

"More coffee?" I asked as I reached for the carafe.

"More of you, Sarah, more of us. This long-distance thing isn't working for us anymore. I need more of you.

I love you, and I want to disagree and make up with you on a regular basis."

"So," he said before I had a chance to say anything. "Hannah and I are in a spot. We need a CEO for the Koenig Group. I don't have time to take it on, and Hannah doesn't have the aptitude or patience for the job. Her business is really growing, and you know she wants to do her own manufacturing, so we need someone dedicated to running things. I think the Inn has a special meaning for you and you relate so well to Hannah. We've had advisors, but she keeps going to you for advice, so we think it is time you were being paid for it.

Of course, it would mean relocating to Hamburg. I'm rattling around in that big house all alone now that Joerg has passed, and Julien is living in Munich. I'd like to share it with you." He paused. "I'm sure you want some time to think about it, but will you consider it?"

I looked out at the sea again and this time it seemed like an endless expanse with no land in sight. The pieces fell into place. The dissatisfaction I was feeling in my life, was because Christian wasn't in it in the way I wanted him to be. I looked across at this man, relaxed and tanned from the sun, and knew that this was what I wanted.

"I don't think I can stand an ocean between us for another minute, Christian."

It only took four months for me to become an ex-pat, as I had employment and a residence to go to. At the end of May, family and friends threw a party, both to celebrate my fortieth birthday and give a *bon voyage* to my new life. Christian and Hannah came for the party, and I joined them in Hamburg a month later.

Dana advised me not to sell my house in The Beaches, so I rented it to a young accountant who had recently joined the firm with the codicil that he and his wife accept my roommate as part of the deal. Zipper was becoming a lazy cat and did not prowl and hunt as much anymore, and I didn't think he could make the move to Hamburg. Doug and Laura had been looking out for him when I was away and, being an equal opportunity roommate, he seems content to fluctuate between the two houses.

I missed my family and friends, but we talked on the phone often. Ro and I talked almost weekly, and in one conversation we reminded each other that we didn't think the type of men we were looking for existed. We were both wrong. She and Joey are very happy with Ben. He stuck to his plan and his business is really taking off. He goes to job sites all over the country, and Ro and Joey go with him whenever they can. Joey has taken to travelling like he was born to it and Ro loves it. Ben hires crews and spends most of his time supervising the jobs and recruiting new ones from Toronto.

My first year went by in a blur. I got a tutor and studied the German language. English is widely used all over Europe, but I wanted to immerse myself in the culture. My tenant in The Beaches keeps me up to date on the happenings at my old firm. He and his wife love the house, and he hinted a few times that they would like to buy it, but I'm not ready to sell just yet. He also regales me with stories of my old roommate Zipper. I miss that fur ball, but he seems to be content with all the attention he gets at my house and from Laura, Doug, and the girls next door.

Hannah was happy to hand over the financial end of her business to me and I love being the Innkeeper of the Koenig Inn. Christian was right, I feel a strong connection to the Inn, and I also love working with Hannah. She is a never-ending source of energy and new ideas, which creates challenges at times, but certainly keeps things interesting. I feel more connected to our projects and hands-on than I had for the past few years in my job in Toronto. Christian is a strong supporter of both Hannah and me, and we rely on his advice, but he does not take a domineering role. I have found the partnership I've always wanted in him.

He converted Julien's bedroom on the second floor of the house in Altstadt into an office for me for when I need quiet time. Dad's ceramic shoe sits on the desk that I now use. Julien decided he wanted to stay in Joerg's bedroom when he visits from Munich.

Julien comes home whenever he can. He will graduate next year and is already being recruited by a few electronic firms in Munich. He tells us that we are moving into the electronic age, and before long we will be connected via the internet, and everyone will carry a cell phone. The three of us talk endlessly about computerizing the shipping industry, but Christian wants him to follow his own path and gain experience and confidence first. Christian is the caretaker, listener, and guide to all of us and he is helping Julien become an extraordinary man.

Hannah is busier than ever doing renovations and designing furniture and fixtures. Dad and Lorna came for a visit, and Dad helped us find a small factory so we could do our own manufacturing. Hannah and I spent months preparing the factory (with Dad's guidance from across the pond) and hiring staff. We are also looking for a retail location where we will showcase and sell works of local artists of all kinds on consignment. With Hannah's connection to the art world in Hamburg, we hired an artsy woman to run the retail store and help me plan events at the Inn.

Mike has taken over the wallpaper and paint division of the business, and his designs and innovative paint colours have been integrated into Hannah's designs. More of his abstract paintings have found their way into Germany, as well as unique furniture designs that we will manufacture and offer in the boutique.

Christian is busy with the shipping business and still goes to sea occasionally. I went with him to England, and we did a crossing to New York in the spring.

"This time we are going to New Jersey, Sarah. We'll see where your father was born."

We sat beside each other at microfiche screens in the library in Jersey City, reminiscent of the day that Dad and I had done the same thing in Hamburg. We scrolled through newspaper articles until I found one that stopped me short. It was a streetscape and the caption stated that it was Dwight Street. I gasped and sat back in my chair. Christian leaned over and looked at my screen.

"It is just as she described it in her journal," he said.

Indeed, it was a long building with stairways mimicking each other all along the street filled with people, women with babies, and children running after a ball and playing games on the steps. The article was dated 1917.

Christian went back to his screen and flipped through more pages as I sat and stared at the picture before me.

"Look Sarah, here is a picture of the harbour, and the article states these are ships returning from Europe after the war."

I put my head on his shoulder and we read the article together. There were pictures of the densely packed harbour, people standing shoulder to shoulder, mostly women, many with small children in hand looking anxiously at the men disembarking from the ships. The men looked like skeletons in ragged clothes and slouched hats. Some were smiling, but many had that vacant expression on their faces as if they weren't quite sure where they were.

He scrolled further and stopped at an article about the Spanish flu. The pictures attached were much different. The streets were eerie and quiet as if the buildings had swallowed up the people. He scrolled on and found a picture of a group of people outside a factory wearing masks over their faces. It must have been summer, as they were in light clothing and looked downtrodden and forlorn.

"Can you imagine wearing face coverings like that all day while working in the heat in those factories?" Christian remarked.

"No, I can't. How could they breathe? They look exhausted," I sighed. "I think I've seen enough, Christian. This is heartbreaking."

"Yes, it is. It was one thing to read about this in your grandmother's journals, but to see these pictures makes it all more real. She certainly captured the essence of it, though, didn't she? I can't imagine living through that kind of pandemic, and hope we never have to." He shook his head at the thought.

"Let's go there, to Dwight Street, and see what it looks like now," he said.

We hailed a cab outside of the library and gave the driver the address. The driver was a man in his fifties with a strong Scottish brogue.

"Do you live there, then?" he asked.

"No, but we knew someone who did many years ago," Christian replied.

"Well, you'll find it much different now," he said. "There is a revitalization program going on in that part of the city and those buildings are being sought after by new people. They are called Brownstones now, and you must have a lot of money to own one to be sure. I've been driving a cab ever since I came to this country twenty-five years ago, and I ain't ever seen anything like it."

We stepped out of the cab in front of number 97 and saw what he meant. The buildings were being sandblasted, taking off years of dirt and grime, revealing intricate architectural features. We stood there for several minutes, both thinking about what my grandmother must have experienced the day she arrived here with Carlos.

Christian took my hand and we walked along the street. There was an open house at one of the stairways and we decided to go inside. We were met at the door by a woman realtor garishly dressed, wearing makeup she must have used a trowel to apply. She had jewel-encrusted glasses hanging on a string around her neck that she put on to look us over closely. She must have decided we were good candidates as she swung into an aggressive sales pitch. Her interest waned when we explained we were visiting from Germany but made a last-ditch effort saying perhaps we would like a residence here for future visits. We ignored her, and she moved on to another couple that arrived behind us. We wandered through the home marvelling at the restoration work that had been done but also thinking about what it must have been like housing small apartments or flats.

Sneaking out to avoid any further contact with the realtor we wandered around the area to see if we could find where Sophia, Maria, and the cousins had lived, but there was no evidence of any small houses with tiny yards. The streets were covered with apartment buildings, high-end shops, and restaurants, catering to the type of people that now occupied that part of the city.

Later we had dinner at one of the restaurants.

"We must tell you father about this," Christian said. "I think he would like to come here sometime to see it for himself."

I nodded. "Thank you for bringing me here, Christian. You are right that my grandmother described this so well in her journals, but it was something else to see it for ourselves."

I brought the box with my grandmother's journals, letters, Lorna's tapes, and notebooks with me to Germany. Christian had read them, listened to the tapes, and shared them with Hannah. He must have discussed our New Jersey experience with her as well.

A few weeks after our return to Germany, the three of us were having dinner at the Inn one night when Christian and Hannah said they had an idea.

"We want to enlarge the picture Joerg had found of your grandmother serving coffee in this room and name it the Ava Baehr room."

They asked for my permission to do so and said they also wanted to call Dad to discuss it with him. We called him later that night and told him what we had found in New Jersey, and he did agree that he would like to see it for himself. He was speechless with shock when Christian presented the idea, he and Hannah had discussed with me, but we both gratefully accepted.

Chapter Twenty-Nine

FAMILY

On a morning in August, my second year in Germany, Christian woke me very early. Groggy with sleep I asked him what was happening. He said it was the fourth anniversary of the day we met.

He left the bedroom and came back with four dozen red roses, a large envelope, and a cardboard box. Sitting up in bed I watched as he set the roses on the bureau and put the envelope on the nightstand and the box on the bed. He sat beside the box and laughed as I shrank back when it moved.

"Go ahead, open it," he said.

Rubbing the sleep out of my eyes, I carefully opened the box. The most gorgeous pair of blue eyes looked up at me helplessly accompanied by a small squeak. I carefully lifted a beautiful white Persian kitten and held it up to my face. She squeaked again, and I noticed a ribbon tied around her belly.

"Here, let me help with that."

I held the kitten out to Christian, and he untied the ribbon which held a small box. I put her on my shoulder, and she snuggled against the side of my face with her soft downy fur.

Christian opened the box and showed me a stunning diamond ring.

"Will you consider being my wife?" he asked.

"Yes, I will consider it," I replied as he placed the ring on my finger.

The kitten squeaked as Christian and I shared an embrace. He then picked up the envelope from the night table and handed it to me.

It contained a Shareholder Agreement transferring forty-nine percent of the shareholding in the Koenig Group to me. Hannah also has forty-nine percent, while Christian retained two percent for himself. I gasped and stared at him.

"All those years you helped people, including us, run their businesses, now it is time to have ownership in one."

"But the Koenig Group includes the Inn," I said with emphasis.

"I know," he replied meaningfully.

I had to wait to call people, due to the early hour and time difference, but that didn't stop me from calling Ro. What are best friends for?

"Sarah? Is something wrong?" she asked when she answered the phone in the middle of the night.

I laughed. "I have news that I just couldn't wait to tell you."

"Wait, I'll go downstairs so I don't wake Ben and Joey," Ro said coming awake.

"Sarah that is the best news ever!" she shrieked when I told her that Christian and I were getting married.

"Oh, I left the receiver open in the bedroom; Ben must have heard. He wants to talk to you."

Ben came on the line and congratulated us. I held the receiver so that Christian and I could both talk to him. I could hear Joey talking to Ro.

"Joey's up, too and he wants to talk to you."

"Sarah, we were looking at the atlas last night and we're only going to be six inches away from you and Christian." I could hear Ro and Ben laughing in the background.

"Oh Sarah, we have news, too," said Ro. "We've been dying to tell you, but we had to wait until everything was settled."

"What, Ro, what? Tell me."

"Ben has a contract in Switzerland and the three of us will be living there for a year. He has good people looking after the jobs in Canada, so he feels comfortable taking this opportunity. I'm taking a sabbatical from the school board and will homeschool Joey. I couldn't say anything until Tom agreed to us taking Joey out of the country for that long, but it's all worked out now. Tom agrees it will be a great experience for Joey, and he and his wife Grace will come for a visit while we are there."

"We'll be close, six inches away according to Joey! We will be able to see each other often while we are there.

Joey is over the moon about living in Switzerland and he is so excited to be close to you and Christian. He misses you! He is the perfect age. We'll be there in mid-September. Promise me you will wait to get married until we get there! You are planning to ask me to be your Matron of Honour, aren't you?"

"Of course, Ro, this is perfect!"

Christian and I were married in the garden at the Koenig Inn on September 30th. I used my grandmother's wedding ring for the ceremony. I had thought about it, but it was Christian who suggested the idea. We took it to a jeweller for cleaning and polishing and chose a gold ring for him. Unknown to me at the time, he had the rings engraved with the word 'family' paying homage to the fact that we were not only marrying each other and becoming a family but also to our families both with us and those who had passed away.

Hannah helped me shop for my dress, even though I was afraid she would want something more extravagant than my taste. But as a skilled designer, she has the talent to know what's right for her client and she found the perfect dress for me. It was a floor-length sleeveless sheath in ivory-coloured silk. I wasn't sure, but as soon as I tried it on, I knew it was perfect. I was tanned from a summer of being outdoors and on the sailboat, so ivory worked well, and the fabric felt fabulous against my skin. It was tailored in such a way that it draped beautifully from a stylish bodice and moved smoothly when I moved. It had a wrap in the same silk fabric in the event of a cool day.

I also borrowed a long-braided gold chain that had belonged to Hannah's grandmother Julia, providing another link to family. It was the right length and weight for the style of the dress and paired nicely with the gold bangle bracelet Christian had given me on our first Christmas together.

My 'something blue' for the wedding was everything else. Hannah took over the decorating and the dining room was turned out in pale blue linens, dishes with tiny forget me not flowers around the edges, and hydrangeas in shades of blue, white, and yellow on the tables.

Ro and I talked almost daily during the remainder of August, both filled with excitement about the wedding and their stay in Switzerland. They had numerous details to sort out, and Ro was busy with a supply teacher who would take her place for the year she was away. They were also looking for a tenant for her house, but she was worried about what to wear as my Matron of Honour. She asked for details about my dress and colour scheme and arrived with a stunning long dress in a beautiful shade of blue that was perfect in every way.

The project that Ben was working on was situated an hour outside of Bern and an agency had found them an apartment on the main floor of a house centrally located in the city where they were within walking distance of everything. Ben was not starting the project until early October, so they settled in and came to Hamburg a few days before the wedding. Family and friends from Canada started arriving and booked into various hotels around the city.

Our friend Martin and the chef from the Inn agreed on the menu for the meal and *hors d'oeuvres* to be served after the ceremony, but a huge argument broke out regarding the selection of wines. Christian had to step in between the two hot-headed chefs, but other than that we had very little to do and spent our time visiting with Ro, Ben, Joey, and our other Canadian guests.

Hannah arranged for a hairdresser and make-up artist who joined Ro and me in one of the bedrooms on the second floor of the Inn to prepare for the wedding. Ro and I are not big makeup girls, and we insisted that we didn't want extravagant hairstyles, but the professionals assured us they knew what they were doing if we would only stop fidgeting and let them get on with it. Of course, that only made us giggle all the more.

The hairdresser did some magic with my hair that made it shiny, and bouncy, and brought out the highlights in the chestnut colour as it fell to my shoulders. She looked at Ro's tangle of curls and mumbled in German, but the end result was just as fetching. Hannah ordered bouquets for us in shades of blue with hints of yellow and white baby's breath, tied with blue ribbon.

The men had boutonnieres in the same flowers. She was about to bring the bouquets to us when Lorna asked if she could.

"You girls look absolutely beautiful," she said her eyes growing moist, but we both cried out,

"Don't start or we will never get through this!"

She kissed us both and scurried down the stairs where my father was waiting.

"Just wait until you see them!" she said holding a handkerchief to her face as she hurried out to the garden.

Julien was acting as the best man for his father and stood beside Dad at the bottom of the stairs. He kissed me as he handed me a German coin to put in my shoe, for good luck. Ro took his arm and they headed to the garden as well. Dad smiled.

"We've come a long way, haven't we Sarah?"

"I know," I said with a lump in my throat as I kissed his cheek.

Christian and Julien were both dressed in beautifully tailored suits, crisp white shirts, and fashionable ties. Christian wore his grandfather's cufflinks. Julien wore the black onyx cufflinks that had belonged to Joerg.

The officiate was a retired judge and lifetime friend of the Koenig family. Ro cried beside me as Christian and I took our vows, as I had during her wedding with Ben. After our kiss as husband and wife, I threw my bouquet, and it was time to party. Julien hugged me tight, welcomed me to the family, and quietly told me that Joerg had hoped I would become his daughter-in-law someday.

Waiters arrived with trays of wine and *hors d'oeuvres* and people started to mingle. The Canadian friends had not seen Julien since Ro and Ben's wedding and the girls crowded around him raising eyebrows at me at the changes in him. I smiled and nodded. Christian and Hannah had invited friends and colleagues and it didn't take long before everyone started to mix.

Martin had been banished from the kitchen and soon found himself chatting with Mike and Marc. They were staying in Europe and doing a culinary/wine tour of Italy. They were also planning to visit our factory and Hannah introduced them to friends in the art community who were pleased to meet the young Canadian artist who was making his mark in Germany. Joey was soon great friends with Dave and Sherri's children. They all wanted to sample the wine, Joey declaring that if he was going to live in Europe for a year, he'd better get used to drinking wine.

Dana took my arm as we climbed onto the front porch where guests were sitting in groups chatting. With her keen eye for real estate she said, "What a fabulous house!"

I laughed. "Who would have thought that I would end up here?"

"Sarah, you were meant for something like this. We all knew that you were different and destined to do something grand with your life."

Ro joined us and said, "Remember the day we sat on your porch in the Beaches, Sar, and talked about the exotic places we would go one day?"

Dana laughed and said, "Who can keep up with the two of you!" as she put her arms around both of us. "It won't be the same without you."

A waiter announced that dinner was about to be served and requested that people make their way into the dining room. I was accustomed to seeing the picture of my grandmother hanging stately on the wall between the two large windows, and Dad and Lorna had seen it on their previous visit. But I watched as my brothers, Ro, and Ben took note of it. Julien knew the story, too but no one else was aware of its significance. It was a family story, and we were content to keep it that way.

The dinner was a success and even Martin was nodding his approval. A small tear appeared on Dad's cheek as he stood to propose a toast. He was funny and touching—my father, always my father, but my good friend as well. I felt my grandmother looking down at me from her picture on the wall and felt an overwhelming sense of gratitude.

Martin arranged a brunch the following day for the Canadian guests. He seated us on the patio away from the other diners and prepared an amazing array of dishes. Everyone was chatting comfortably about their plans for an extended stay in Europe. John had behaved himself at the wedding but was relaxed and his comical self again.

"Frogs will never be the same" he sighed. "Sarah went off to become an entrepreneur and an Innkeeper, of all things; and now she's gotten married. And Ro will be roaming around Europe for the next year. Has anyone asked me how I feel about all this?" He placed his hand over his heart in mock distress. "You two have been my best targets for years. I may have to resort to pulling people in off the street!"

"At least your jokes will be new to strangers," said Katie. "We've heard them a thousand times."

"Well done, Katie, well done" exclaimed Ro." Who knew what a smartass lurks under that yuppie exterior."

Christian took my hand under the table as everyone laughed. He knows these people mean the world to me; they welcomed me with their friendship and offered me a soft place to land during times of chaos and confusion, even if they didn't know what I was going through. He also knew the previous year together provided time for me to adjust to a new living/working life in Germany and for our relationship to develop. I squeezed his hand

and smiled. We are partners and confident that together we will face whatever challenges the future may bring.

Later everyone was milling around while the big round table was cleared and dessert and coffee were offered. I noticed Hannah in conversation with Dave and his family. Christian and I joined them. "What are we talking about?" he asked. "Natalie was telling me about her French Immersion program at school and her interest in languages. I think she should come to Germany to finish high school and expand her resume. I know the Director of an excellent private school that would be happy to have such a bright young student." Dave and Sherri were stunned by the suggestion but Natalie was delighted with the idea.

Christian and I glanced at Julien, who was chatting with Ben. He would graduate university the following spring and, whatever he chose to do beyond that, he was no longer a boy.

"That's a great idea, Hannah!" Christian exclaimed. "Natalie could live with us; we have lots of room and would love to have a young person around." Christian, the caretaker; I smiled, nodding my agreement.

Later, Ben and Ro announced that they had to leave to catch their train to Bern. Julien was taking the afternoon flight to Munich, and slowly the party started to break up with hugs, a few tears, and more of John's jokes.

Christian and I had plans to spend the rest of the week at home. We had both been working hard for months and wanted some downtime. We slept late, cooked meals together, and sat in Joerg's garden enjoying the last of the warm weather. The staff at the Inn delivered the wedding gifts to the house and we spent an afternoon at the dining room table taking our time opening each gift, and writing thank you notes. We had dinner with Mike and Marc at Martin's restaurant before they left for Italy and talked about the designs he had left with Hannah.

Katie called on the weekend. She and Ian were flying back to Canada while Dad and Lorna were taking a bus tour in southern Germany and into Austria.

We chatted about their trip and the things they had done.

"Sarah, we didn't want to steal your thunder last weekend, but Ian and I just found out that we're expecting. We told Mom and Rauf about it this week."

"Oh, Katie, congratulations! Lorna must be over the moon!"

"She is but worried about me flying. I'm in my first trimester and my doctor gave me the go-ahead. Other than being a bit nauseous, I feel fine, but that could be from all the German food we've been eating."

We laughed. "I want to tell you Sarah how happy my mom is with your father. They are so good together and this trip has given us a chance to get to know your dad. She was lonely, and now the two of them are making all kinds of plans."

"Dad is happy, too, Katie and you know how fond we are of Lorna. She will be the world's best grandmother."

EPILOGUE

IT IS SUMMER again and I am working at my desk in the house in Alstadt. It was late afternoon and I had been crunching numbers for hours. I tucked a few wisps of hair into the ponytail on top of my head and stood to stretch. The window was open, and I could hear birds at the feeder and feel a soft breeze. I leaned against the window frame, absently twirling my grandmother's gold ring on my finger.

The kitten Christian gave me on the day he proposed is now a grown cat, beautiful and pampered. She had been curled up on a chair snoozing while I worked. She padded over to join me at the window. "Did you have a good nap, Pearl?" I asked picking her up and petting her soft fur.

Julien joined us for Christmas at a chalet in Switzerland with Ro, Ben, and Joey. The guys went skiing while Ro and I drank hot chocolate beside the fire and talked for hours. Christian and Ben hit the slopes, but Julien spent time on the beginner's hill with Joey. He became Julien's shadow after that and followed him everywhere.

Ben bought Euro rail passes when they arrived in Switzerland, and they spent their free time travelling. Occasionally Ben would have to stay on the job site for a few days and Ro and Joey would hop on a train and visit us in Hamburg or I would go to Bern and join them on short trips to Lucerne or wherever they were going. When Ben had a break, the five of us travelled through France for a week. Ben's project is complete, and they will be leaving in a few weeks. Joey will start high school in September and is growing up much too fast. Christian and I are going to Bern on the weekend to say our good-byes. We will miss them terribly but are making plans for Christmas in Toronto.

Dad and Lorna are an established couple. They kept their own residences in Toronto but spend a lot of time together and travel often. Lorna spends the winter in Florida with Dad where they golf, swim, play bridge, and visit with friends when they aren't entertaining family. Lorna's sister-in-law, Margery, bought a house in their community so her children and grandchildren also make the exodus to Florida.

In the spring Dad and Lorna flew to Calgary and took the train through the Rocky Mountains to Vancouver to visit Lorna's son Daniel and have plans to motor east in September to the Maritimes, with a stop in Montreal.

Dave and Sherri took the kids to Florida during the March school break. They spent a few days with Dad and

Lorna on a side trip to Disney World. According to Brad, their next stop will be Disney Land in California. After many family discussions and telephone interviews with Hannah's friend on the School Board, Dave and Sherri finally agreed that Natalie would come to Hamburg for her final year of high school. She immediately enrolled in night school at the Community College to learn German and is doing a six-week course at summer school. Dave and Sherri agreed to cover the cost of the private school but said she will have to earn her keep and help us at home. She said she would be delighted to work on a part-time basis at the Inn, boutique, or retail store and her biggest help to me will be with the German language. She will be coming to Hamburg at the end of August and will travel with us to Toronto to spend Christmas with her family. Christian is right; it will be fun to have her with us.

We went to Munich for Julien's graduation in the spring and he started his job with the electronics firm in Munich. He only managed one trip home since last Christmas, and his free time will be limited in his new job. We talk often and support him in his career and are still hoping he will find his way into the family business when the time is right.

Mike's furniture designs are being manufactured in the factory and selling well in the retail store. Hannah wants to add upholstered chairs to the line, and he has supplied some wonderful designs for fabric. He continues his graphic art business and abstract paintings, but about twenty-five percent of his work is for the Koenig Group.

Katie and Ian surprised us all with twin babies, Benjamin, and Abigail. They sent pictures and our favourite is one of Dad and Lorna, each holding a small bundle and wearing beaming smiles.

John was offered the position of Fire Chief in Guelph. Dana got a real estate license and connected with a contractor building houses in the south end of Guelph. He is convinced that Guelph will become a bedroom community for Toronto, and she is selling his houses as fast as he can build them. She is studying for a broker's license and plans to open her own firm.

Our other firefighter friend Dean was not able to attend our wedding as he suffered an accident in a house fire when the second story collapsed, and he fell through breaking his leg in several places. He underwent months of intense therapy but worked hard and is now back on the job. My co-worker from the firm, Linda, decided it was too stressful being with a firefighter and their relationship ended. She left the firm and now practices tax accounting in a firm in Oshawa.

My tenant in the Beaches became even more adamant that he and his wife wanted to buy my house. I had resisted. The Beaches is a very special place to me; I believe I became an adult during my years there. I had lost my mother, found my father, and built stronger relationships with my brothers there.

My tenant was my link to the accounting firm, where I had worked hard as an independent woman and had proven my worth. But things were changing there, my former boss was retiring, and Linda was gone. Christian did not try to influence my decision but was supportive as always. In the end, I decided to sell my house in the Beaches. I had formed lasting friendships in the Beaches, but John and Dana were gone; Katie and Ian had moved to a bigger suburban family home with their twins. Ben had worked on a few projects in Alberta and would be starting a new one there in the fall. They liked the mountains and lakes of Alberta, even more so after their year in Switzerland.

Ro had committed to returning to her school in the Beaches and they wanted Joey to settle into life in Toronto again, but they talked about buying a condo in Calgary. Ben could use it as his base when he was there and it could be a holiday spot for Ro and Joey, for now. My friends were going in different directions, but that is only geography. I am confident these friendships would continue, especially with Ro, Ben, and Joey.

I heard the door open and footsteps down the hall to the kitchen. A few minutes later Christian appeared in the doorway.

He leaned over for a kiss and said, "Wow, you really did need some quiet time," taking in the mess of spreadsheets and other documents on my deck.

"I'm starting to go snow blind, so it's time to quit for the day. The Inn has been so busy with weddings since early April, and we are booked every weekend straight through the fall. I think we started something with our wedding last year."

He smiled at me.

"Indeed, we did," he said. "I'm cooking, will you be much longer?"

I pulled him in for another kiss and said, "No, not long."

He tickled Pearl under the chin, pulled my ponytail and left for the kitchen. I turned to look out the window again as a soft breeze ruffled Pearl's fur against my skin. "He's the best, isn't he?" I said to my beautiful furry friend. She looked at me with her gorgeous blue eyes and seemed to smile in agreement.

AUTHOR'S NOTE

THANK YOU FOR reading *Pearls on a String.*

Pearls On A String is a work of fiction. Living with Covid 19 these past few years has changed lives worldwide. Many have died in this pandemic, but many more have been saved through advances in medicine, science, and technology. Our planet is a small place and we know what is happening with people in our lives, wherever they may be and can meet with them visually over social media. Through 24/7 news streams, we are informed of world events the minute they happen. We can work from home and shop over the internet. PTSD, disabilities, sexual orientation, mental health, social assistance, and human rights are all part of a normal conversation.

It was much different in the past. Millions of lives were lost to the Great War of 1914-1918 and the Spanish flu that followed. Millions more were changed forever. We are all descendants of the brave survivors who carried on as best they could, but they were not encouraged to talk about it. The burden of their past died with them and many of their stories have never been told.